LOCKED IN

LOCKED IN

MARCIA MULLER

GRAND CENTRAL
PUBLISHING

NEW YORK   BOSTON

Grand Central Publishing
Hachette Book Group
237 Park Avenue
New York, NY 10017

Visit our website at www.HachetteBookGroup.com.

Printed in the United States of America

First Edition: October 2009
10 9 8 7 6 5 4 3 2 1

Grand Central Publishing is a division of Hachette Book Group, Inc.
The Grand Central Publishing name and logo is a trademark of Hachette Book Group, Inc.

Library of Congress Cataloging-in-Publication Data
Muller, Marcia.
    Locked in / Marcia Muller. — 1st ed.
        p. cm.
    Summary: "After being shot in the head, Sharon McCone suffers from locked-in syndrome, which involves almost total paralysis but an alert conscious mind. As Sharon lies in her hospital bed, furiously trying to break out of her body's prison and discover her attacker's identity, all the members of her agency fan out to find the reason why she was assaulted"—Provided by publisher.
    ISBN 978-0-446-58105-9
    1. McCone, Sharon (Fictitious character)—Fiction. 2. Women private investigators—Fiction. I. Title.
    PS3563.U397L63 2009
    813'.54—dc22   2008051426

For Bette Golden Lamb,
with many thanks from her honorary medical person
and
Bill,
for a story that started out as a joke

MONDAY, JULY 7

SHARON McCONE

A typical July night in San Francisco. Mist swirling off the bay, a foghorn bellowing every thirty seconds out at the Golden Gate. Lights along the Embarcadero dimmed, and the sidewalks and the streets mostly empty at a few minutes after nine. Sounds of traffic on the Bay Bridge curiously muted. In contrast, my boot heels tapped loudly on the pavement.

Ahead of me lay Pier 24½. Three long blocks behind me my vintage MG sat in a no-parking zone, out of gas.

Way to go, McCone. When you fly, you're meticulous about fueling. But with the car, you resist stopping at a station till the damn thing's running on fumes.

Just my luck—the fumes had given out short of my destination tonight.

Pilot error—on the ground.

A sudden blast of wind came off the water, and I gripped my woolen hat, pulled it lower on my forehead. Something to my right was banging, metal on metal: I glanced over and saw a NO TRESPASSING sign loosely attached to a chain-link fence barring access to one of the old piers scheduled for demolition.

This is my workday neighborhood. I walk this lovely, palm-lined boulevard all the time. I shouldn't allow sounds to spook me.

Another moan from the foghorn. Why did it sometimes seem melancholy, at other times strident, and at still others like the scream of a victim in pain?

Now I was passing a derelict shed on the far side of the doomed pier. A heap of rags lay on its loading dock. No, not rags—a human being seeking shelter from the inclement weather. Another member of San Francisco's homeless population.

One of many things wrong with this damned city—too few resources, too little compassion.

I had a love-hate relationship with the town I'd made my home. But I knew, no matter how bad the urban situation became, I'd never leave.

Ahead the security lights of Pier 24½ glowed through the mist. I quickened my steps.

The city's port commission had tried to raise the tenants' rental rates last fall—a first step toward also demolishing this pier—but an influential attorney friend of mine had prevailed upon them to maintain the status quo. For a while, anyway.

Where, I wondered now, would I find a comparable rate and space for an agency that was growing quickly? Profits were up, yes, but salaries and the cost of employee benefits were also escalating. Maybe . . .

I put my worries aside and concentrated on my original purpose: retrieve the cell phone that I'd accidentally left on my desk before going out to dinner with one of my friends and operatives, Julia Rafael. The phone whose absence had prevented me from calling Triple A when the car ran out of gas. If I contacted them from the office, they'd be there by the time I walked back to the MG—

A hand touched my forearm. I jerked away, moving into a defensive stance. A dark figure had loomed out of the mist.

"Lady, can you spare a dollar?"

Jesus, he was panhandling in a nearly deserted area in *this* weather? Better to fort up in the shelter of one of the sheds, like the person I'd glimpsed earlier.

He waited, arms loose at his sides, shoulders slumped. I couldn't see his features, but the wind whipped at his jacket and I saw it was thin and had a ragged tear.

I reached into the pocket of my peacoat and found some bills that I'd left there whenever I last wore it. Held them out to him. He hesitated before taking them, as if he couldn't believe his good fortune.

"Thank you, lady. God bless."

He disappeared into the fog as swiftly as he'd appeared.

I pulled the collar of my coat more tightly around my neck and went on toward the pier.

The powers that be say you shouldn't give money to the homeless; they'll only spend it on drugs and liquor. What was that slogan they made up? *Care, not cash.* All shiny and idealistic, but the truth is, some people slip through the cracks in the care department, and cash for a bottle or a fix is what they need to get themselves through a cold, damp night like this one.

I thrust my hands deeper into my pockets, but a chill had invaded me that couldn't be touched by the warmth of wool and lining.

The fog seemed thicker now. It played tricks on my vision. Someone was coming at me from the bayside. . . . No, advancing toward me on the left . . . No, there was nobody—

A shriek echoed over the boulevard, high-pitched tones bouncing off the surrounding buildings.

I stopped, peered hard through the churning mist.

Laughter, and the sound of running feet over at Hills Brothers Plaza. More laughter, fading into the distance along with the footsteps. People clowning around after leaving one of the restaurants.

The security grille had been pulled down over the yawning, arched entrance to the pier. My opener was back in the MG. I grasped the cold bars and called out to Lewis, the guard we tenants collectively employed.

No answer.

Well, sure. He was probably drinking in the far recesses of the cavernous structure. Or already passed out. A nice guy, Lewis, but a serious alcoholic. At the last tenants' meeting we'd talked about firing him, but none of us had taken the initiative to find a replacement. I should have—

That's not your bailiwick any more, McCone. You've got Adah to take care of things like that now.

Adah Joslyn, formerly of the SFPD's homicide detail, now my executive administrator. Last winter I'd stepped back from the day-to-day running of the agency so I could concentrate on cases that really interested me. There hadn't been many, and in the meantime I'd started giving self-defense classes at a women's shelter in my neighborhood and working their emergency hotline during the day when most of their volunteers were out earning a living. I'd been able to spend more time at Touchstone, Hy's and my seaside home in Mendocino County, and at our ranch in the high desert country with our horses, King Lear and Sidekick.

I shouted again for Lewis.

Still no answer.

Damn. I'd have to use my security code to open the door to the right of the pier's entrance. But I'd just changed it, as we did every month, and I wasn't sure. . . .

Favorite canned chili. Right. I punched in 6255397—the numerical equivalent of NALLEYS on the keypad—and gained entry.

Usually there were cars belonging to tenants parked on the pier's floor at any time of day or night: employees of my agency, the architectural firm and desktop publisher on the opposite catwalk, and the various small businesses running along either side of the downstairs worked long and irregular hours. Tonight I was surprised to find no vehicles and no light leaking around doorways. The desk where Lewis was supposed to be stationed was deserted.

That does it. We're firing your ass tomorrow.

I crossed the floor to the stairs to our catwalk, footsteps echoing off the walls and high corrugated iron roof, then clanging on the metal as I climbed up and went toward my office at the bayside end. God, this place was spooky at night with nobody around.

As I passed the space occupied by my office manager, Ted Smalley, and his assistant, Kendra Williams, I thought I saw a flicker of light.

So somebody was there after all. Maybe Ted had left his car on the street; if so, he could give me a ride back to the MG. Kendra took public transit; she could keep me company while I waited for Triple A, and then I'd drive her home. I went to the door, calling out to them. No response. I rattled the knob. Locked.

I'd imagined the light. Or it had been a reflection off the high north-facing windows.

I went along to my office, slid the key into its dead-bolt lock. When I turned it, the bolt clicked into place. Now that was wrong; I'd locked it when I left the office. We all made a point to do so because we had so many sensitive files in cabinets and on our computers.

I turned the key again and shoved the door open. Stepped inside and reached for the light switch.

Motion in the darkness, more sensed than heard.

My fingertips touched the switch but before I could flip it, a dark figure appeared only a few feet away and then barreled into me, knocked me against the wall. My head bounced off the Sheetrock hard enough to blur my vision. In the next second I reeled backward through the door, spun around, and was down on my knees on the hard iron catwalk. As I tried to scramble away, push up and regain my footing, one of my groping hands brushed over some other kind of metal—

Sudden flash, loud pop.

Rush of pain.

Oh my God, I've been shot—

Nothing.

THURSDAY, JULY 17

SHARON McCONE

A thin bright line. Widening. Slowly. Beige light.

What . . . ?

My eyes began to focus.

A ceiling. I'm on my back looking at an unfamiliar ceiling.

A tube was thrust into my mouth, and from somewhere nearby came a rhythmic breathing sound. In my peripheral vision were other tubes, snaking in many directions. Metal bars to either side, like a baby's crib.

I couldn't move my head either to the left or to the right.

Straight ahead, a curtain. Beige and green—a leafy pattern.

Rhythmic beeping sounds from behind me.

Hospital room. I'm in a hospital!

But where . . . ? What . . . ? How . . . ?

The light dimmed, narrowed—

The light returned, softer now.

Rustling noises and then, in profile, a face.

Nurse? Must be. Blue scrubs and a gentle, placid expression. Asian, probably Filipina.

She moved away.

Come back! I need to ask you—

Everything dimmed again.

*   *   *

Dark now, but a shaft of light slanting across the ceiling. Must be coming from a doorway. Faint sounds of men and women talking. No, one man and two women. Who . . . ?

Hospital staff. A friend had once told me hospitals were noisy at night; no cessation of activity then. Nurses gave medications, responded to emergency situations and the ring of patients' call buttons.

Call button . . .

It would be within easy reach. All I had to do was feel around for it—

My right arm wouldn't move.

My calves and feet hurt, an ache that went straight to the bones. I couldn't move them either.

Paralyzed!

No, that can't be.

Frantically I willed some part of me to move—a finger, a toe, anything.

Nothing.

Total immobility.

A scream rose in my throat. A scream without voice.

I couldn't make a sound.

What's happening to me?

Cold, foggy night along the Embarcadero . . . Derelict coming out of the mist . . . Deserted pier . . . My office . . . Shadowy figure slamming into me . . . Flash, pop, pain . . .

Oh, God!

Panic shot through me. The scream rose to a high, shrill pitch, but only in my mind.

". . . Appears comatose. As you know, it took quite an effort to stabilize her." A stranger's voice, grave. "But her blood pressure is finally in hand, essentially normal, she's taking nourishment through the feeding tube, and is able to breathe well on her own since we began taking her off the ventilator yesterday."

"Do you have a definite diagnosis yet?"

Hy! But what—?

"Traumatic brain injury, of course, but beyond that we can't yet say. The CT scan shows the bullet entered the occipital lobe of her brain, carrying along with it bone fragments. A clot formed from internal bleeding, creating pressure."

"And the prognosis?" Hy's voice was tightly controlled, but I knew he was quaking inside.

"Too early to tell. It's—if you'll excuse my wording—a mess in there, which is why we can't attempt surgery. She appears comatose and completely paralyzed, but the scan we took yesterday shows she has good brain wave activity."

"So she'll come out of this?"

A pause. "I do think you may have to face some hard decisions about your wife's quality of life." Rustling of paper. "I see here that you have her advance directive giving you medical power of attorney. Have the two of you discussed her wishes?"

"Yes." Curt. He wasn't ready to go there yet.

I'd been listening to the conversation dispassionately, as if they were talking about somebody else. Now my defenses crumbled, and I gave in to panic. The silent scream rose again.

The doctor said, "Have you given any further thought to transferring her to the Brandt Neurological Institute?"

"I spoke with them this morning. They have a room available and will admit her as soon as you give the go-ahead." Hy hesitated. "Isn't this the equivalent of giving up on her?"

"Not at all." The doctor's voice was too upbeat. "It's an excellent acute rehabilitation center. Dr. Ralph Saxnay, who will be her attending neurosurgeon, is one of the best. In addition, it's very quiet and private. No one needs to know she's there." A pause. "You must realize we've had difficulty with the media here. Your wife has made quite a name for herself in this city."

Hy didn't respond to the doctor's comment. "I'll make the final arrangements with the institute."

Final arragements. It sounds as if he's planning my funeral.

The doctor said a few more things in low tones, and then I heard him leave the room. Hy was still there, standing back and to the right of me; I couldn't see him.

I tried to say something, to move something again. Couldn't do anything. Paralyzed.

But not in a coma as the doctor had said.

Hy doesn't know. I can't communicate with him, even though I can hear every word he says.

Hy sighed heavily and placed his hand on my forehead. "Oh, McCone, I don't know if you even realize I'm here." His voice was twisted with pain.

Look at me! Look into my eyes! You'll see I'm with you.

"If you can hear me, remember that I love you. Hold to that thought, and we'll get through this together. Just like we always have."

I love you too, Ripinsky.

HY RIPINSKY

He stepped out into the parking lot of San Francisco General Hospital and turned up his collar against the fog. Walked toward where he'd left his silver-blue 1966 Mustang, fumbling in his pocket for the keys. When he got to the classic machine, he had to curb a violent desire to kick it. This was not the time to give way to impotent rage.

Not yet, anyway.

Inside the car, he took out his cell phone and called the Brandt Neurological Institute's admitting office. He told the clerk he'd arranged for his wife's transfer, then set up a meeting with Dr. Ralph Saxnay, the neurosurgeon, for eleven the next morning. After he ended the call, he just sat there, staring out at the gathering mist.

Nothing more to be done today. Shar would be in good hands tomorrow. Not that there was anything wrong with SF General's trauma unit—they'd saved her life with all the odds against her—or ICU; they were both excellent, but they'd done all they could and weren't set up to handle a patient with a long-term . . . condition.

His thoughts flashed back to his first wife, Julie, now many years dead of multiple sclerosis. Toward the end she'd also been unmoving and silent, but there'd been an absence about her, as if her essence had already left her body. Not so with McCone; he still felt the psychic connection that had bound them together since almost the first time they met. If she was beyond all hope, would that connection exist?

No, he refused to believe it.

The past ten days were a jumble in his memory. His shock when the call came to his hotel in Seattle from Ted Smalley, who had been summoned along with the police and paramedics when the half-drunk security guard found McCone shortly after hearing the shot. The frantic and reckless flight to San Francisco piloting Ripinsky International's jet. Heart-pounding drive from the airport, where two days before he'd left the Mustang inside the jet's hangar, to the hospital. Then the waiting, a three-day and -night vigil.

We've established a good oxygen supply ... Blood flow and pressure returning to normal ... A setback, blood pressure crashing ... BP edging toward normal ... She's responding to the medications ... Another setback, incompatibility with the medication ... Have to be very careful with meds in cases of traumatic brain injury ... No, we can't operate at this point; chances of her survival would be very slim. ...

Why don't you get some rest. Mr. Ripinsky? Really, you'll be no good to your wife if you don't rest.

Of course, he hadn't rested. Had sat by her bedside, alert for any change, any sign. And later, when they'd said she was stabilized, he'd stayed with her in the ICU except for brief trips home to shower and change and field phone calls from her family and friends.

Her adoptive mother near San Diego had collapsed upon hearing the news and been placed under sedation, according to Sharon's stepfather. Sister Charlene and her husband, Vic, were in the city, in spite of Sharon's not being allowed visitors. Calls came daily from her birth mother in Boise, Idaho; from her birth father on the Flathead Reservation in Montana; from her half sister Robin in Berkeley; from her sister Patsy in Sonoma. Brother John arrived from San Diego and installed himself in Sharon and Hy's guest room.

The people at the agency knew better than to bother Hy. They had established a rapport with two of the floor nurses who kept them posted.

Hy leaned forward and grasped the steering wheel, weariness and helplessness diluting his earlier rage. When he'd first heard the news of McCone's shooting, the rage had been dominant: he'd flown the jet recklessly, driven erratically, burst into the hospital like the proverbial storm. Now he was wearing down, the only bright spot on the horizon being the slim hope that the Brandt Neurological Institute promised.

Life without her—

No, for God's sake, don't go there!

He straightened, grasped the wheel.

So what to do to pass the long evening? Go home, where everything was a reminder of Shar, and their cats stared at her favorite chair with bewildered eyes? Where her brother John would rekindle his rage with endless discussions about "getting the bastard that did this"? Go to the RI office, catch up on paperwork in the hope it would numb his mind enough to let him sleep on the sofa there? Impose his presence upon friends who had already done more than he could ever repay?

None of the above.

He started the car and drove toward Pier 24½.

Cars were parked on the pier's floor—so many that he had trouble slotting the Mustang. Odd, this late in the afternoon. Some of the offices on the first story were closed, but lights blazed upstairs at McCone Investigations, and he sensed tension and activity. As he climbed the stairway to the catwalk, he heard voices coming from the conference room.

When he appeared in the doorway, silence fell. Adah Joslyn, Sharon's executive administrator, broke it by saying to Hy, "Is there—"

"No news. She's being transferred to an acute care facility tomorrow."

A collective sigh of disappointment mixed with relief. No news was bad news; no news was good news.

"Am I interrupting something?" he asked.

"No, no, of course not. Come in."

He did, taking a chair against the wall, since there were no places left at the round oak table.

Adah was standing: an elegant, slim woman in a well tailored navy blue suit, with a honey-tan complexion and beautifully corn-rowed black hair. The perfect image for an increasingly successful agency, just as she'd been the perfect image for the SFPD's campaign to promote women and minorities—not only because she was female, but because she was also half black and half Jewish. The perfect image until working the homicide detail had taken its toll and Shar had made her an offer she couldn't refuse. In spite of Adah's tightly controlled exterior, Hy knew her to be funny, generous, and a thoroughly staunch friend.

The silence stretched out. He said, "Go on with whatever you were discussing, please."

Looks were exchanged around the table. Adah said, "Actually, we should have invited you to this meeting, Hy. It's kind of . . . a tribal war council."

"Meaning what?"

"We're Sharon's tribe . . . family . . . whatever—"

"And we're pissed off, going to find out who shot her," said Sharon's nephew Mick Savage.

Hy turned his gaze to Mick. The petulant, spoiled son of a country-music superstar had matured into a stand-up man in the years he'd known him. Hard to grow up in the shadow of his father, but Mick had managed—in spite of being a tall, blond version of handsome Ricky Savage, but without his father's musical talent, ambition, or ruthless drive. Mick had found both his present and his future in computers and, owing to the revolutionary software programs he was currently creating with fellow operative Derek Ford, would someday rival Ricky in fortune, if not in fame.

Hy said, "So how do you intend to nail this person?"

The operative who replied surprised him: Julia Rafael. She and his wife had had dinner at a Mission district tacqueria before Shar had returned to the pier to pick up her forgotten cell phone. Julia was something of an engima to Hy. She'd worked the streets of the Mission district from age twelve, selling herself and drugs. Arrests, abortions, and the birth of a son whose father she couldn't begin to name had followed. The boy had given Julia a purpose; after her final release from the California Youth Authority, she'd turned her life around.

Hy, ever distrustful of dramatic turnarounds—in spite of having made one himself—had waited for Julia to screw up. And when she was arrested for crimes that put Sharon's license and the agency in serious jeopardy, he'd wanted to say "I told you so." But Julia, vindicated, had turned into a fine operative. He still wondered at McCone's friendship with her: Julia was insecure in the extreme and covered it with a haughty, sometimes hostile demeanor. But McCone was an excellent judge of character, so she must have seen gold in Julia that was yet to be mined.

Now Julia said, "We started on these investigations the day after Shar was attacked, with the idea that the shooter had to have some connection with one of the cases the agency was working. Otherwise why was he skulking around the pier at night?"

"He wasn't looking for money or stuff to sell for drugs," Adah added. "Nothing was taken."

"Unless Shar interrupted him before he could take something," Hy said.

"It's possible, but this has more the feel of an instrusion by somebody who knew the pier, knew Lewis was a drunk and likely to leave his station for long periods of time. Your average thief doesn't just walk into someplace with a lighted guard's desk."

"Or shoot his way out of the situation if he's caught," Julia said. "He'd hide—unless he was afraid Shar would recognize him."

"Someone who had been here before, then," Hy said. "Someone she'd seen. Not necessarily her client, but one of the agency's, or a witness or suspect in one of the cases."

Adah nodded. "That's our reasoning. Anyway, we did an in-depth analysis of all cases going back two months. There're a number that raised red flags. We've eliminated some, but there are several that still hold our attention. Why don't you tell us about yours, Julia?"

"Okay. There're two of them, both cases where the SFPD

dropped the ball. Haven Dietz was the victim of a violent knifing attack a year ago that left her disfigured and with only partial use of her right arm. The other clients are the Peeples, Judy and Thomas. Their son, Larry, was gay. He disappeared suddenly six months ago. No satisfaction from the cops in either matter."

Hy asked, "What're the red flags?"

"Dietz and Peeples were friends, lived in the same building. He cared for her while she was recuperating. She was the one who recommended us to the parents. I sense there's something she's not telling me—about Peeples or her attacker."

Adah said, "Let's move on. Mick?"

"Have you heard of Celestina Gates?"

Hy shook his head.

"Identity-theft expert. Had a syndicated column and regularly appeared on national talk shows advising people how to safeguard themselves. Trouble is, two months ago her own identity was stolen. When the media got hold of the situation, they ridiculed her, questioned her credibility. The syndicate canceled her column, a book deal fell through, and the talk-show offers stopped coming in. Red flag is that I sense something wrong with the whole situation."

"That's it?" Hy asked.

"That's it. But Shar would feel the same. When something's off, we have similar instincts."

Hy couldn't debate that. Sharon had a shit detector that seldom failed her.

"Rae?" Adah said.

Rae Kelleher, the then-assistant whom Sharon had brought with her from All Souls Legal Cooperative when she established her own agency. Red-haired, freckled, blue-eyed, and petite. A part-time operative and author of three crime novels. Married to Mick's father, Ricky Savage. Ricky and Rae were Hy's and Sharon's closest friends. No way she wouldn't wade into this mess, ready to do anything she could to help.

"The Bay Area Victims' Advocates is the client," she said, looking directly into Hy's eyes. "They're concerned with getting solutions to unsolved crimes against women. This one's a homicide, back-burnered by the SFPD. I'll give you a copy of the file."

"Thanks."

Adah said, "Craig—your turn."

Craig Morland was Adah's significant other. A former special agent with the FBI, he'd become disillusioned with the federal agency and was eventually lured away from DC to San Francisco by Adah. When they'd first met, Craig had been a buttoned-down, shorn, and shaven man with—as Hy had characterized him—a stick up his ass. No one would confuse his former persona with that of the easygoing, tousled-haired, mustached man of today.

"I'm looking into corruption at city hall. Big-time chicanery, but I can't yet figure out on whose part. My informant is very close with the information. Till I've gone into it further, I'd rather not reveal details."

Hy said, "Hey, man, we're talking about my wife getting shot."

"And if it's connected to this case, we're talking about maybe more people getting shot. People close to us." Craig paused. "I need a couple more days. Okay?"

Hy shrugged, suddenly feeling bone-tired.

The meeting broke up then, people standing and gathering their things as if on cue. Rae's hand pressed his arm. "Come to our house and spend the night," she said. "I know it's hard to go home—especially with John there. John is not soothing when he's angry."

"That's understating it."

She urged him to his feet. "Lasagna and a feather bed—that's what you need."

"The hospital—"

"Will call you if there's any change. Right now you come with me."

He went. Lasagna and a feather bed sounded good. It would be better if he could share both with Shar, but that wasn't going to happen.

Not tonight. Maybe not ever.

FRIDAY, JULY 18

SHARON McCONE

They had removed the tube from my mouth for good yesterday, and now were disconnecting the patches that connected me to the monitors from my arms, legs, and chest.

God, those are my lifelines! They're going to kill me!

The voiceless scream rose. Subsided when someone said, "Okay, let's get her onto the gurney."

Being lifted. Moved sideways. Down onto a harder surface. Tugging of blankets. Clicking of strap connectors.

Where are they taking me? More tests?

I struggled to make my vocal cords work. Couldn't.

I tried to raise my arm. Couldn't.

Clumsy maneuvering through a door. Then swift forward motion, wheels bumping over uneven spots on the floor. Acoustical ceiling and fluorescents passing overhead. Automatic door noise, and then . . .

Fresh air. Cool and faintly salt-tinged.

I'm outside!

Another voice: "We'll take her from here." A face appeared above me—male, smooth, young. "Ms. McCone," he said, "if you can hear me, I'm Andy with the Sequoia Ambulance Service. We're taking you to the Brandt Neurological Institute."

Oh, right. Where Hy told the doctor he was having me transferred.

The terror subsided, and I blinked my eyelids, but Andy had

looked away. "It's only a twenty-minute trip," he added, "and we'll try to make you as comfortable as possible."

Why does he sound as if he doesn't believe I can understand a word he says?

Will somebody please look at me and see I'm still here?

Weariness washed over me and I slept.

Cool light. Blue walls. Scent of fresh-cut flowers. A window. And beyond it a thick stand of eucalyptus.

I love eucalyptus. I wish the window were open so I could smell them. But this floral scent . . . what . . . ?

I tried to look around, but from the way the bed was positioned I couldn't see much more of the room. Looked up. Suspended from the overhead track was a stainless steel contraption that looked like an elaborate, multi-barbed fishhook. An IV bag was suspended from it, as well as a container of a brownish liquid.

Alone? Yes, I can tell by the quality of the silence.

Tired. So tired. Was it yesterday that Hy said it had been ten days? Ten whole days since I'd been in a coma, then weak and helpless?

No, admit it—paralyzed.

But not in a coma. I can think, see, hear, breathe, and feel. I just can't move or speak.

Just? That's everything!

Got to find some way to let them know.

Got to!

Someone coming into the room. Hand on my forehead. Hy.

"We're at the Brandt Institute, McCone," he said. "I just met your new neurosurgeon. They're going to do everything they can to help you."

Don't stand over to the side. Look at my face!

"It's a nice place, out on Jackson Street, near the Presidio. Nice people, too."

Look at me, dammit!

"First thing tomorrow they're going to run some more brain scans and try to get an accurate diagnosis. Then . . ." He fell silent for a few seconds.

"Hell, McCone, if you could hear me, you'd know I'm clutching at straws here. There's so much they don't know about the brain, and I know even less. God, I can't . . ."

He was crying. I'd seldom known him to cry.

He moved around, bent over, and buried his face on my shoulder. His body shook and his tears wet my hospital gown. I wanted to hold him, and I couldn't move. Comfort him, and I had no words.

After a moment, he raised his head and looked straight into my eyes.

I blinked at him, moved my eyes up and down.

He drew back, astonishment and hope brightening his drawn features. Gently he reached out to touch my face.

"You're here with me!" he said.

I blinked again.

"You can hear me. See me."

Blink.

"Can you move?"

I decided two blinks would mean no.

"Can you talk to me?"

Blink, blink.

"Doesn't matter. You're on your way back. I'm getting your doctor."

Thank God. I knew I could count on you, Ripinsky.

But what the hell took you so long?

RAE KELLEHER

She propped her right elbow on the desk and lowered her forehead to the palm of her hand. Her eyes ached and pain nee-
dled above her brow. Through the open doorway of her study she
could hear her stepdaughters, Molly and Lisa, squabbling downstairs over which DVD to watch. She wouldn't interfere. Let them
duke it out—that was her parenting philosophy. Prepare them
ahead of time for the often rocky shoals of life.

She took several deep breaths. The throbbing stopped. She
raised her head and fumbled in the desk drawer for eyedrops.
They soothed the ache.

She raised her head and stared out the window to the north-
east at the fog-shrouded towers of the Golden Gate Bridge. Below
the house waves pounded the shoreline. Many millions' worth of
view. She remembered when she and Ricky and the real-estate
agent had first toured the multilevel mansion in the exclusive Sea
Cliff area: it was so beautiful that she ached to live there. She'd
been poor and in debt most of her life, and she couldn't believe
anything remotely like that was possible. But in the bedroom with
the indoor hot tub overlooking the sea, Ricky had put his arms
around her and said, "What do you think, Red? Will you live here
with me?" The answer was a given.

Back to the present, she told herself.

But the present was so depressing. Shar . . .

She thought back to her initial interview with the woman she'd hoped would be her boss, when Shar was staff investigator at All Souls Legal Cooperative, a poverty law firm. Rae had been in her twenties, trapped in a bad marriage to a professional student, and adrift as far as a career was concerned. Shar's faith in her ability to make a good investigator had given her the strength to break with her husband and move on. And as they worked together, a friendship strong enough to last a lifetime had formed between them.

At least, she'd thought it would last a lifetime, till some scumbag had pumped a bullet into Shar's brain.

And now she was trying without much success to connect this old homicide to Shar's shooting. Cold cases fascinated most people, but as far as Rae was concerned they were a pain in the ass. For that matter, so was the director at the San Francisco Victims' Advocates. Maggie Lambert, an old-school feminist and former rape victim with great empathy for her mostly deceased clients. But Maggie wasn't interested in providing accurate files or details. She wanted instant resolutions to cases that had been gathering dust forever.

Plus it was hard for Rae to focus when she was so worried about Shar.

Shar—now almost but not quite a relative by marriage. Ricky was only Shar's former brother-in-law, but his and her sister Charlene's six kids—four of whom Rae was participating in raising—had caused her enough trouble to qualify her for family membership. They weren't collectively called the Little Savages for nothing.

Back to the files.

Angie Atkins, in her late teens, a hooker who'd been found slashed to death three years ago in an alley off Sixth Street downtown—San Francisco's skid row. No family, no history. She'd never been fingerprinted—didn't hold a driver's license—but Rae had a lead on another hooker who had been Angie's best friend. So far her informant had only given her a first name—Callie—which she could've made up in order to get the money for her next fix.

Victims' Advocates was a nonprofit group funded by various foundations and state and federal grants. Their focus was on cold cases involving violence to women. Although they employed two investigators, they were currently on overload, and McCone Investigations had agreed to take the case pro bono.

Why, Rae thought now, had she been the one Adah Joslyn approached with the assignment? And why had she agreed? She didn't draw a salary from the agency, didn't need to work if she didn't want to. But although she and Ricky had so much money that neither of them would have to lift a finger for the rest of their lives, idleness wasn't a component of their natures. So he managed his recording company, scouted for new talent, issued an occasional CD, and performed charity concerts. She wrote and investigated, because both pursuits were in her blood.

Now Rae tried to think of scenarios that would link the cold case with the burglar who had rifled their offices and then shot Shar. It was a stretch. She'd asked Patrick Neilan, the operative who coordinated their investigations, to look into those that Shar had been working three years ago. He'd turned up nothing to link with this one.

Finally Rae gave up and decided to have a glass of wine while she waited for Ricky to return from his recording company's headquarters in LA.

Then the phone rang. An informant with an address for Angie Atkins's friend Callie—last name O'Leary.

MICK SAVAGE

He was really pissed off, and Celestina Gates wasn't improving his mood any.

She strode around the living room of her Nob Hill condominium issuing statements that boiled down to it's-all-about-me and why-haven't-you-found-out-who's-ruined-my-life. Tall, willowy, with long dark hair, she normally would have attracted Mick. *Had* attracted him when he'd first met her. Now, instead of taking her to bed, he wanted to dangle her off her twelfth-story balcony.

Being pissed off had to do with Shar's condition: Gates's problem seemed so trivial compared with what had happened to his aunt. His aunt, who had put up with his immaturity, mentored him, given him a sure direction in life.

If this Gates bitch had anything to do with Shar's shooting . . .

He waited with gritted teeth till his client's tantrum had passed, sitting on her red leather sofa and looking at the gray sky above the grim brownstone facade of the old Flood Mansion across California Street—a creation of famed architect Willis Polk that now housed the exclusive Pacific-Union Club. When Gates finally sat in a matching chair opposite him and fumbled with a cigarette and lighter, he said, "Ms. Gates, something's wrong here."

"Of course something's wrong! My life and career are destroyed!"

"That's not what I mean."

Her nostrils flared. "What, you think I'm not telling you everything?"

She'd said it, he hadn't. "Yes, I do."

"How dare you—?"

He held up his hand. "Last night I was rereading the case histories you describe in *Protect Your Identity*. In each one, it took a long time for the individual to regain access to bank accounts and establish new credit card accounts and ratings."

Wary now. "Yes."

"I understand that as an expert on identity theft, this would be easier for you to accomplish than for a run-of-the-mill victim—even one using your book."

"I suppose so."

"Yet you chose to hire our agency."

"Well, sometimes an objective investigator can do a better job than the individual involved."

"Uh-huh. You claim you've been financially ruined."

"I have been."

"This condo—your mortgage is ninety-five hundred and thirteen dollars a month."

"How do you—?"

"And that Jaguar in the garage downstairs is leased for three thousand."

". . . Right."

"Your credit cards are all clean, and over there in the foyer are five big shopping bags full of stuff from places like Gucci and Neiman Marcus."

"So what's your point?"

"You don't seem to be hurting—at least not as badly as you've made it out to be."

"I've tapped into my savings—"

"Your column's been canceled, nobody wants you on TV, clients are running like hell from your consulting firm. And you told me a book contract's on hold. You're spending a lot for someone who's living on her savings and has no prospects for future income."

She stubbed out the cigarette and immediately lit another. "I have an image to keep up."

"According to you, that image is ruined."

"All right, so I'm a compulsive shopper."

"I doubt that. You're too savvy a businesswoman to yield to impulse."

"We all have our faults."

"And one of yours is lying."

"I'm sorry?"

"Never lie to an investigator when you're trying to pull off a scam, Ms. Gates. It's too easy for us to check into your background, credit rating, and finances. I did, when I started feeling uncomfortable about you. Everything's golden, except for a scam you pulled off before you left your hometown in Texas. And that's been pretty well covered up; I had to dig hard for the information. It was a similar scam to the one you're trying to pull off now, but on a more minor scale."

"What the hell—?"

"Failure and triumphant recoveries generate publicity and profits. Your career has been slacking off for at least two years since other, more reliable consultants have come on the scene. My guess is that you hired our agency so you could outshine us by solving your own manufactured identity theft and putting yourself back on top."

She was silent now, glowering. Caught out.

"Who was going to be the lucky individual to take the blame for the theft?"

More silence.

"Well?"

"You're so smart. Who do you think?"

It came to him in a flash. Himself! Why hadn't he realized that before? Dumb, just plain dumb. He was the perfect scapegoat: he had all her significant information, and she'd probably set up a way to prove he'd had it before she ever went to McCone Investigations. Set up a way to prove the nonexistent identity theft, too.

He didn't have to ask her why she'd picked him. Publicity value. After all, he was Ricky Savage's son.

Nearly choking on his anger, he stood and loomed over her. She squirmed a little but maintained eye contact.

He said, "On the night of July seventh, did you or someone you hired go to Pier 24½ looking for information I'd gathered?"

"Me? Why— Oh, God, that was the night your boss was shot!"

"Right."

"I didn't go there. I never hired anyone. You can't involve me in that—oh, no."

Her defensive reaction seemed genuine, made him think she was telling the truth. "I'll accept that for now. But if I find out otherwise, I'll go to the police and the press and expose you for what you are."

"Does this mean you're dumping me as a client?"

"What do you think, Ms. Gates?"

In the elevator on the way down, he thought, I really should've dangled the bitch off her balcony.

CRAIG MORLAND

He waited in the booth of the dimly lighted bar on Peach Alley, not far from the Civic Center.

He felt as if he were meeting Deep Throat, but at least this wasn't a parking garage, so he could get a drink.

The Deep Throat analogy was valid, though: in 1973 and -74 Mark Felt, then assistant director of the FBI, had leaked details of the Watergate break-in to a *Washington Post* reporter and brought down the Nixon presidency. Although San Francisco wasn't Washington, DC, if what Craig's informant had been telling him was true, it could very well blow the lid off city government.

The bar was quiet, even now at the tail end of happy hour; politicos didn't hang out there because there was nobody important to see them and no deals to be made. During Craig's tenure with the Bureau in DC he'd spent a lot of time in lively look-at-me establishments—sometimes on duty, sometimes to impress a date—and he hadn't realized how much he hated them till he'd thrown it all away and moved to San Francisco to be with Adah.

Adah: poster woman for the SFPD, assigned as liaison to the same special FBI task force as he was. Goal: to apprehend a man who'd been bombing foreign consulates. Unused to playing hardball like the Bureau's men, Adah had gone into an emotional meltdown, and Craig had helped her through it. Later, after she'd fully healed, he himself became broken and disillusioned by the work that had steadily eroded all his idealistic dreams, and during coast-to-coast phone conversations whose cost had rivaled the national debt, she'd supported him in his decision to leave the Bureau. Now Adah had given up her similarly disillusioning career with the SFPD, and only Shar's need for an executive assistant had saved them from a move to Denver, where she'd been offered an administrative position at the DPD. Good thing, too: he hated snow.

Thoughts of Adah and the agency immediately turned into thoughts of McCone. It was fucking unbelievable that she was in a coma. That a random—or maybe not-so-random—encounter after hours at the pier could have reduced such a vital woman to a vegetative state . . . Neither he nor Adah had been sleeping much since it happened, and some nights she'd slipped out of bed and he'd heard sounds of crying coming from the bathroom. He didn't cry, but a couple of nights he'd taken out his anger on the refrigerator, pounding its door till his fist was bruised—which, for him, amounted to the same as tears.

Craig looked up as his informant came through the door, swept the room with wary eyes. Spotted Craig and moved toward him, looking stupid in a hat and trench coat. Did he really think no one would notice him?

Harvey Davis was the former campaign manager for Amanda Teller, president of the city's board of supervisors, and one of her most trusted aides. Independently wealthy, handsome, sophisticated—in spite of tonight's silly disguise—he had recently been voted one of the city's most eligible bachelors by a national magazine. He'd contacted Craig three weeks ago, claiming something was very wrong at city hall.

"What'll you have?" Craig asked as the man sat down.

"Scotch, neat. Single malt."

"Done." He went to the bar and ordered. When he returned to the booth and set the drink down, he asked, "What've you got for me? You haven't given me much so far."

"She's meeting with Janssen on Saturday."

She: Amanda Teller. He: Paul Janssen, a state representative for this district.

"Where?"

"Down the coast. A rundown lodge near Big Sur."

"Why Big Sur?"

"Good halfway point: Amanda's giving a talk at UC–Santa Barbara Friday evening. Besides, the lodge is isolated and no one's likely to recognize them there."

"So what's this—about sex, power, money?"

"Not sex, I don't think; they reserved separate rooms—under false names, of course. Power and money? For sure. What else? Who knows?"

"You're not giving me a lot to go on."

"It's all I have. How's your boss doing?"

"Still in a coma."

"Too bad. McCone's a good woman."

"Yeah, she is."

Craig's informant tossed back what was left of his drink, stood up, and slid a piece of paper across the table. "Here's the information on Teller and Janssen's meeting."

"Thanks."

"I also want to give you a key and the security code to my condo."

"Why?"

"Evidence there. Videos. If something happens to me . . ."

"What, you mean—?"

"Just take the key." He placed it on the table. "The security code's 1773. I'll be in touch."

Craig pocketed the key, watched him go, and after half a minute, followed him.

The street was deserted, dusky, fog-damp. Davis's footsteps echoed off the pavement down the block. Craig went the other way toward his SUV, fumbling for his keys. They caught inside his jacket pocket and he had to pause to extricate them.

Behind him Davis's footsteps stopped. Craig glanced back, saw him unlocking the door of a white Mercedes sedan. Davis looked at him, gave him a thumbs-up sign, and got into the car.

Finally the keys came free. Craig again started walking toward his SUV. Davis still hadn't started the Mercedes; he was a methodical man and was probably making minor adjustments to the seat and mirrors—as if they would've moved in the brief time he'd been in the bar.

Craig was halfway around to his driver's-side door when a vehicle started up, its engine burbling as if something was wrong with the exhaust manifold; it pulled out from the curb across from him, nearly grazing his front quarter panel. Black pickup with a white camper shell. The driver had forgotten to put on his lights—

Craig whirled, shouting after the truck, but it kept going toward the end of the block where Harvey Davis's headlights were flashing on.

A gunshot echoed loudly in the narrow street.

Instinctively Craig dropped to the pavement, his hands protecting his head.

Two more shots, staccato bursts. Semiautomatic weapon, he thought. The pickup's tires squealed as it sped around the corner onto Golden Gate. Harvey Davis's car stayed in place, its engine purring in the sudden quiet.

Knowing what he would find, Craig pushed to his feet and ran toward it.

JULIA RAFAEL

S he looked across her desk at Haven Dietz and said, "I'm sorry I asked you to come in so late in the day, but there're some things about your case I need to check out."

A jagged scar extended from below Dietz's right eye to her chin, another across her brow. Although you couldn't tell it unless she moved, her right arm was useless because tendons and muscles had been severed during the knife attack last year. Before that, according to Julia's file, Dietz had been pretty and confident, a junior executive with a top financial management firm. Now her blonde hair hung lank and unwashed; she wore no makeup; she seemed shrunken inside her baggy sweater and jeans, as if protecting herself against further attack. She had other scars that you couldn't see, but they were psychological and emotional.

Pobrecita.

Julia always thought in her primary language when she was upset. And every time she conferred with Haven Dietz, she had trouble concealing her emotional turmoil.

Thing was, it could've been her. Was more likely to have been her, given her past. She'd been hooking and dealing on the tough streets of the Mission district when she was a teenager; Haven had been assaulted while taking a shortcut home through a park in the supposedly safe, middle-class outer Richmond district.

Por Dios . . .

But something wasn't right with Dietz, and Julia couldn't pin it down. She'd come to the agency for help, but her behavior ranged from noncooperative to hostile. Also, she professed to dislike Larry Peeples's parents, yet she'd strongly urged them to contract with the agency and request Julia as their investigator. Of course the cases were connected, and Dietz knew it.

Always before, Julia had met with Dietz at her apartment, but today she'd asked her to come here. Power play.

"I'm finding strong links between your case and the Larry Peeples disappearance," Julia added. "Can we talk about your relationship with him again?"

The woman sighed and fired up a cigarette without asking—in spite of the NO SMOKING signs posted on the wall along the catwalk. "We've been over and over this. Larry was a neighbor and he was gay. We were casual friends, nothing more."

Julia didn't like Dietz, but more than once she'd told herself she couldn't let it interfere with her investigation.

"You and Larry were close friends, according to his lover, Ben Gold."

She shrugged. "We lived on the same floor. Sometimes I'd go to dinner at his apartment, or he'd come to mine. We didn't exactly run in the same social circles."

"When you saw him, what did you talk about?"

"Haven't we done this before?"

Julia bit the tip of her tongue to control her temper. "It helps to keep going over things."

Another sigh. "We talked about my job at the firm and his at the Home Showcase. About movies we'd seen and books we'd read. Nothing heavy. It was a way to pass the time and not have to cook for one. I don't exactly call that a relationship."

"But Larry took care of you when you came home from the hospital."

"Nobody else was going to." Bitterness filtered into her tone. "My parents were too busy sailing their damn yacht across the Pacific. My so-called friends turned out to be people who couldn't deal with disfigurement."

Dietz looked down at the cigarette, which was close to burning her fingers. She registered that there was no ashtray on the desk and glanced around.

"We don't encourage our clients to smoke," Julia said and motioned to her wastebasket. "Make sure it's out. The service's already emptied it, but I don't want the plastic bag to melt."

Dietz ground the butt out on the basket's side and dropped it in. The smell of scorched plastic immediately drifted up to further poison the air.

Julia said, "You've told me you and Larry didn't see too much of each other after you recovered from the attack."

"No, we didn't. He was working extra hours at Home Showcase and was with Ben Gold a lot. Besides . . ."

That was one thing she'd been holding back.

"Besides?"

"Well, we had kind of a falling-out. He told me I was a terrible patient and didn't appreciate all he'd done for me. I offered to pay him for his time, and then he called me a spoiled rich brat. Which is definitely not fair, because if anybody was spoiled it was Larry. His family has tons of money: they own an award-winning winery in the Sonoma Valley."

Julia knew all about the winery: Larry's grieving parents had told her that shortly before he'd disappeared he'd agreed to return home and train to take over the business. They'd also invited her up there for a tour and lunch, but so far she hadn't gone. She didn't know how to act or dress in social situations with rich people. Across her desk she did better.

She said, "You and Larry never made up, right?"

"Right."

"But you suggested that his parents consult our agency about his disappearance."

"That was to get them off my back. They kept coming down here and hammering me with questions. They're sure I know something—which I don't."

Julia consulted her file. "The day Larry disappeared—"

"We've been over this at least half a dozen times. . . . Oh, hell, all right. I ran into him at the mailboxes about eleven that morning. We ignored each other. Later I felt guilty about that. After all, he did take care of me, and I'm *not* a very good patient. Besides, the building manager had told me Larry was giving up the apartment and moving back to Sonoma. So after I went out for groceries I went over there to say good-bye. He didn't come to the door, although I sensed he was there, so I said the hell with it. Two days later Ben Gold came to my door asking if I'd seen Larry. And then the police got into it, and then the damned parents."

"This Ben Gold—what's your take on him?"

Dietz shrugged.

"Come on, you must've formed some opinion." From her background check, Julia had learned the details of Gold's life: born in the Bronx to a poor family; abusive home life; tried to make it on the New York stage and, when he didn't, headed to less competitive San Francisco, where he'd had modest success with low-budget commercials. But she really couldn't get a handle on Gold, other than that he was very distressed by his lover's disappearance.

"He doesn't like me, and I don't like him," Dietz said. "He's ambitious about the acting and modeling. Sucked up to Larry's parents, too. Have you talked with him?"

"Yes."

"So what's *your* take on him?" Dietz asked.

"For a while he wasn't getting on with his life. Spent a lot of time at the Peepleses' vineyard. The mother seems to view him as a substitute for her son. That's about to end, though; he's moving to LA soon—something about an acting job."

Dietz's brow knitted and her gaze grew far away. After a moment she said, "Those parents . . ."

"What about them?"

Another shrug.

"Why d'you suppose they think you know more than you're telling?"

"You'll have to ask them."

Julia had more questions, but her phone rang. She checked to see who was calling and said, "I need to take this."

HY RIPINSKY

He slumped in a chair across the desk from Dr. Ralph Saxnay, Shar's attending physician at the Brandt Neurological Institute. The starkly white and functional office was very quiet, except for the ticking of a grandfather clock on the facing wall. City sounds were muted in this eucalyptus-surrounded enclave.

"Mr. Ripinsky?"

"I'm sorry. It's difficult to process all this."

"I understand."

Hy studied Saxnay. The doctor was tall and thin and totally bald, with a pale skeletal face and small blue eyes. Intelligent eyes, and full of compassion.

The situation with McCone was evidently much worse than when the medical professionals had thought she was in a coma.

"I don't understand why nobody noticed she was . . . in there," Hy said. "Shouldn't they have seen the eyeblinks and motion when they put saline solution or whatever it is they use to keep the eyes hydrated?"

"Initially she was in a coma; if the patient's eyes are closed and hydrating normally, there's no need to augment it. Anyway, now that we know she's awake, as indicated by the good brain wave activity shown in the CT scans taken at SF General and here earlier today, our preliminary diagnosis is locked-in syndrome. Do you know what that is?"

"No."

"Have you seen the film or read the book *The Diving Bell and the Butterfly*?"

"Neither."

"Well, then. The syndrome is caused by traumatic brain injury: head wounds as in your wife's case or by stroke. Before you leave today, we'll provide you with literature that may help you understand it more thoroughly. And, of course, there's plenty of material on the Internet, although much of it may be inaccurate. With locked-in syndrome, unlike coma, the patient has normal sleep-and-waking cycles, is conscious, can think and reason, and has sensation throughout her body. Your wife can blink and move her eyes and, now, breathe without a ventilator—all of which are very positive signs. But, as you know, she cannot speak or move or take nourishment without a feeding tube."

It was a moment before Hy could process the information. "What's the course of treatment for this syndrome?"

"We will take measures to prevent infection or pneumonia and give her physical therapy to prevent her limbs from contraction. She'll be turned often to prevent bedsores. Good nutrition will be provided, of course. A speech therapist will help her to establish a communication code utilizing eyeblinks or eye movement."

Alarm seeped into him. Something the doc wasn't saying.

"And the recovery time . . . ?"

Saxnay met his gaze evenly. "The mortality rate is high. Patients typically die within months, although some live for a few years."

Months. A few years.

No! Not McCone!

". . . You're saying she'll never come out of this."

"No, I'm not, Mr. Ripinsky. The syndrome is relatively rare; there's a lot we don't know about it. Medical science is developing new methods such as implanting electrodes in the brain which bypass the normal communication channels from the brain to the muscles. Most of these are still in the experimental stage, but as soon as they're proven, we'll try them. Ms. McCone is a strong, otherwise healthy woman in full possession of her intellectual faculties. Each case is different—"

Yeah, yeah, yeah. Let me tune you out now. Because what you really mean is that my wife is going to die in silence.

She's going to die, and there's not a damn thing I can do to prevent it.

Now Saxnay left him alone for a while, ostensibly to collect more test results on Shar but really, he knew, to allow him to regroup. The grandfather clock ticked—seconds of his wife's life slipping away. He got up and paced around the office.

All those times he and McCone had cheated death. The explosion in Stone Valley. The ambush down on the Mexican border. The near-crash in the Tehachapi Mountains.

And by herself: all the stuff from the past she'd told him about. Last year, when she left RKI's Green Street building seconds before it blew up. Last November, when a lousy rental plane had crapped out on her and she'd had to crash-land in the high desert.

And now a fragmented bullet was lodged near her brain stem, doing more harm than all the criminals and aeronautical malfunctions could. A deadly little piece of metal, that none of her smarts and guts could combat.

RAE KELLEHER

The rundown Tenderloin district on the edges of the city's posh downtown had improved since she'd first moved to San Francisco, but there were still more bad areas than good. Barred storefronts, boarded-up windows, winos passed out in doorways. Every stripe of predator on the prowl. But she wasn't afraid. She'd walked these streets after dark many times before and come out unscathed. And she'd had the good sense to get firearms-qualified with a carry permit while she was Shar's assistant at All Souls. Tonight she was armed and alert for danger.

A hooker in a short skintight red dress gave her the evil eye.

No, sister. Do I look like somebody who's trying to take over your turf?

A man in a black leather jacket and pants, accessorized with flashy gold jewelry, surveyed her speculatively, then looked away.

Well, I'm not a target for pimps, at least. Good to dress down for this foray.

She slowed at the corner of Ellis and Larkin, checking the numbers of the buildings on Ellis. Proceeded to the middle of the next block. The place where she was headed was one of those old brick six-story jobs that had once been respectable apartment houses and were now transient hotels—a polite term for flophouses.

She pushed the door open and went into a grubby faux-marble entry whose mailboxes had been vandalized, their doors ripped off or hanging on bent hinges. The entry opened into a dimly lighted lobby with a desk to one side, where a white-haired man sat in a chair, his head bent forward, chin resting on his chest. Snores gusted from his mouth.

She tiptoed past him to the elevator. Out of order. She looked for the door to the stairs, took them to the second floor. Room 209 was to the right, in the back.

She knocked on the door, called out softly, "Callie?"

No answer.

"Callie?" Louder.

Nothing.

This was definitely the address her informant had given her on the phone for Callie O'Leary, friend of the murdered hooker, Angie Atkins. So where was she? Out on the streets? With a john someplace else? Having dinner?

Of course, it could also be a bogus report, so the informant would seem to be doing the job Rae had paid her for. Or a trap of some kind. Well, let anybody try something: she had less than a hundred dollars in her purse, as well as her nine-millimeter Glock.

She slipped the Glock out, then turned the knob. The door wasn't locked, and it swung open into a pitch-black room. No sound, no motion, no odor except disinfectant. She edged inside, found a light switch, flipped it on.

Empty.

Just a small room—couldn't have been more than six by nine— in a state of disorder. She moved toward a pair of doors and, with the Glock in her hand, pulled one open. A bathroom, towels on the floor, mildew in the shower; the other gave into a closet full of empty hangers.

Shit. If Callie O'Leary had lived here, she wasn't just away for the evening, she'd cleared out.

Rae took out a pair of surgical gloves and snapped them on. Went back to the door to the hallway and closed it. Set the lock and secured the chain. Then she began to prowl.

Bedclothes rumpled and twisted, covered with stains she didn't care to inspect. Pair of laddered pantyhose thrown over the room's one chair. Ashtray full of lipsticked butts beside the bed; Callie's choice of smokes was Virginia Slims. Bureau: nothing but a worn-out pair of red crotchless panties. Bedside table drawers: only a few packages of condoms and a phone book.

She took the book out and turned to the first page. People often noted things down there, and Callie had been no exception. In rounded handwriting were the words BILL DELANEY—CELL, 415-555-6789.

Rae ripped the page from the book, took another look around the room, and left. When she passed through the lobby, the elderly clerk was still snoring.

MICK SAVAGE

W e can eliminate Celestina Gates," he said. "In fact, I'd've
liked to do it with my own bare hands."

Patrick Neilan, freckled face lined with weariness, red hair tousled from many finger-combings, asked, "Why?"

"The woman is a total asshole. A fraud, too." He filled Patrick
in on his meeting with the identity-theft expert. "Just a publicity
stunt."

Patrick consulted the large flowchart on the wall of the office
he shared with Adah, wiped out the Gates line of investigation.
"So we can assign you to help somebody else?"

"Sure. Derek's got the computer forensics stuff in hand." Derek
Ford: a tall, slender Eurasian man of about Mick's age. Always expensively attired and well groomed—one of those males the press
had termed "metrosexual." Mick and Derek were close friends and
had developed some awesome software programs together. They'd
be millionaires when they licensed them, but neither had any in-
tention of quitting investigating or tinkering with new concepts.

"Let's see where we're at." Patrick got up from his desk, consulted the chart. "Julia's cases—interesting. The vics knew each
other, parents of one are involved. Rae's—dead hooker. Kind
of open-and-shut, but the Victims' Advocates won't let go of it.
Craig's thing with city hall—I don't think he'll let you in on it."

"Well, let's see about that."

"I'll talk to Adah. She's the boss woman for now. You got anything going for tonight?"

"I did—woman I met at the health club. She bailed."

"*You're* going to a health club?"

"Yeah. Partly as therapy, partly because I'm trying to avoid the clubs." Mick had been in a serious, drunken motorcycle accident last November—the culmination of a binge that started when his live-in love, Charlotte Keim, left him. Broken bones and a ruptured spleen, plus two surgeries, had taught him one of life's big lessons. Charlotte had taught him another: in spite of rushing to the hospital to comfort him, she wasn't coming back.

"What about you?" he asked Patrick.

"Pizza night with the boys." Patrick was a single father, with sole custody of his sons.

"Exciting lives we lead, huh? You seeing anybody?"

"Are you kidding? The only people I'm seeing are the other parents at PTA and the kids' teachers. I hang around the laundry place down the street hoping somebody new'll come in and change my future."

"Could be worse for both of us. At least you can go out for pizza and I can work out."

Patrick's face sobered. "Yeah, God, Shar . . . You know, she hired me because she'd done a job locating me for my greedy junkie ex and felt bad about it. And she helped me get custody of my boys. She even cosigned on a new car when my old one died. I owe her."

"So do I. We've got to nail whoever shot her."

"Well, we'll be working on it all weekend. I'll let you know what Adah says about your reassignment."

"Thanks." Mick got up and left Patrick's office. The loneliness of an empty Friday night came over him, and he decided to head for the Brandt Institute: maybe Hy needed company.

CRAIG MORLAND

He watched from among a crowd of onlookers at the end of the alley as the police and paramedics arrived.

If Davis had documented the information he'd passed along to Craig, the shit was about to rain down.

Craig slipped away from the rubberneckers into the darkness on Golden Gate, where he'd moved his SUV before the area became crowded. He had an hour, maybe less, to get to Davis's fortieth-floor condo in One Rincon Hill, which at sixty stories in the main tower was the tallest residential building on the San Francisco skyline.

The South of Market district—once known as South-of-the-Slot—had long been an undesirable industrial area on the wrong side of the Market Street cable-car tracks. Now it was upscale, with luxury mid- and high-rises luring affluent young professionals as well as empty nesters from the suburbs where they'd raised their families. Craig had heard various names applied to SoMa: Mid-Market, Transbay, Rincon Hill, and Mission Bay. Each had its own character and price tag, but all were known for proximity to fine dining and cultural attractions, as well as killer views of the city and bay.

He found a parking space on Harrison, a block from One Rincon Hill, and hurried toward the high-rise building while pulling on a baseball cap that shaded his features. It could be tricky getting around the doorman, but as a former FBI agent he was used to playing tricks. One of the number of cards he kept in his wallet identified him as Walter Russom of Ace Couriers. He flashed it at the man, explaining that he had to pick up a rush delivery from Harvey Davis. The doorman was the trusting type: he let Craig in and motioned toward the elevators.

Craig had met with Davis at his condo only once, on the day Harvey first asked him to look into the malfeasance at city hall. Davis hadn't wanted to meet at the pier; someone might recognize him and word could get around. At the time, Craig had thought him paranoid. He didn't any more.

The hallway of the fortieth floor was deeply carpeted, the walls well insulated. Someone was playing the piano at the opposite end from Davis's condo, but the sound was faint, soothing.

Craig took out the key Davis had given him, unlocked the door. Punched the code into the keypad, then shut the door and rearmed the system. He waited, allowing his eyes to acclimate to the darkness.

Short hallway ahead, with louvered doors opening into what must be closets. He moved along, alert, listening for someone else's presence. The hallway ended in a spacious living room. The lights from the surrounding buildings and the Bay Bridge were spectacular. Craig turned away from them, went down another hallway to the den where he'd met with Davis.

The den was a middle room that backed up on the outside corridor; no windows, so he felt safe turning on a light. He began with the desk, sifting through the files and papers in its drawers.

Nothing.

Videos . . .

No file cabinets. Closet—empty.

Back to the living room. Big entertainment center, but aside from a few movies with political themes, the only discs were from Netflix.

So where were these videos Davis wanted Craig to take in case something happened to him?

Where would *he* put them?

Bathroom, bedroom, closets. Nothing.

Kitchen, seldom used judging from the contents of the fridge and cabinets.

Seldom used, except the man had owned a large selection of spices, which were lined up in wood-bracketed rows in a deep drawer. So many spices that Craig, a fairly good cook, hadn't heard of most of them. Hibiscus powder, zhug, ajwan seed—and not a one of them with the protective seal broken.

Why was it that a deep drawer seemed so shallow?

He began removing the jars. The bottom that they rested on was a different kind of wood from the drawer itself. He pried it up.

Two DVDs.

He pocketed them.

A buzzer sounded. Intercom from the doorman.

The police were there. He had to get out now.

He rushed to the door and down the hallway. Went through the exit to the stairs and waited. Elevator arriving. Footsteps and the doorman's voice proclaiming, "Told me he was from some courier company. Urgent pickup, but he never came down. What the hell's going on?"

Craig took advantage of the confusion and the absence of a gatekeeper to escape the building with his evidence.

JULIA RAFAEL

The phone call she'd interrupted her conversation with Haven Dietz to take was from Ted, sounding upbeat.

"Jules, McCone's conscious, but there're some complications. Hy asked me to schedule a staff meeting for first thing in the morning."

"Complications?"

Dietz glanced up at the sound of alarm in Julia's voice.

"Look, I can't explain now. I've got a lot of other calls to make. Try to get to the meeting no later than eight."

"Will do." From the way Ted sounded, the complications couldn't be too serious. Of all of them at the agency, he'd known Shar the longest and been most optimistic about her recovery.

Dietz looked at her questioningly as she hung up the phone. "A problem?"

"Yeah. Nothing that concerns your case."

The woman scowled, reached for her cigarettes, then thought better of it.

"So what else do you need to ask me?"

Julia leaned back in her chair, wishing she could go home to her ten-year-old son, Tonio, and her older sister, Sophia. Over the past year her income had risen enough that Sophia could retire from her job clerking at Safeway, but still it wasn't fair to stick her with so much of the housework and childcare.

Her cellular rang again. Would the calls ever stop so she could get on with this?

Judy Peeples. "Ms. Rafael, I'm so glad I got hold of you. We— Tom and I—were wondering if you could come up to Sonoma this evening."

A long drive—at least an hour and a half. Julia closed her eyes and let a sigh slip out.

"I know it's an inconvenience," Mrs. Peeples's high-pitched voice went on, "but we'll have a late supper waiting for you, and a nice guest room. You see . . . we found something."

"What did you find, Mrs. Peeples? Something of Larry's?"

"Well, yes. No. It's hard to explain."

"Please try."

". . . Tom was in the tack room—"

"Tack room?"

"A room off the stables where we keep equipment."

"I see. Go on."

"What he found . . . it had to have been Larry that put it there, because it's certainly nothing that any of the workers would've hidden and we've never seen it before."

"What is it, Mrs. Peeples?"

"Cash. A lot of cash."

"How much cash?"

"I don't think I should say any more about it on the phone. Please, Ms. Rafael, will you come?"

Mierda. The woman sounded desperate. "All right. I'll be there as soon as I can."

After she closed the phone, she looked at Haven Dietz. The woman was staring at her. "Larry's mother?" she asked.

"Right."

"They found something? Cash?"

"I'm afraid what she told me is confidential."

"But our cases, you say they're linked—"

"That doesn't mean you have the right to information from my investigation for the Peeples—any more than they have a right to information about yours. We're going to have to continue our conversation later. Tomorrow night at your place?"

"Fine with me." The woman got up from the chair and moved toward the door in a slightly off-balance walk.

Julia sighed, glad to see her go. Then she picked up the phone and dialed home. No reading the next installment of *Robinson Crusoe* to Tonio, no having a glass of wine and talking over their days' events with Sophia. And in her jeans and hoodie she wasn't dressed for a late supper in the wine country, although she did have the necessities of an overnight stay in a travel bag in the trunk of her Toyota; Shar had taught her to be prepared for trips out of town.

When Sophia answered, she told her where she was going and asked her to kiss Tonio goodnight for her.

The job came first. Always. Another thing Shar had taught her.

SHARON McCONE

*T*onight I'm feeling cold and so alone.
 Cold, in spite of these thermal blankets tucked solidly around me.

Alone, not just because Hy's gone now, but because after our eyes met and he realized I was still here with him, he met with my doctor and then he was distracted and sad the whole time he was in the room.

Something wrong. I know. I can feel it. My emotional senses are sharpened, while my physical sense of touch is practically nil. When someone touches me, I'm aware of it, but when no one's there it's like being suspended in still air.

To think that I might never respond intensely to Hy's touch again—that is the most painful.

I had wanted to ask him so many things before: How was he doing, now that he knew I wasn't a total vegetable? Had he reassured family and friends? How were our cats, Ralph and Alice? The agency—how was it running?

And most important, who the hell had shot me?

No, that wasn't most important. I wanted to know exactly what was wrong with me. What it would take for me to survive this . . . whatever the condition was.

I felt trickling wetness on my cheeks. Normally I would have licked the tears away and told myself I was being self-indulgent. Now I couldn't move my tongue, and self-indulgence seemed like a luxury I was entitled to. I ached to turn over and bury my face into the pillow and sob.

Nurses on rounds. Subdued voices. Pretty brown-haired Latina woman smiling down at me, adjusting tubes, checking my vital signs, smoothing the covers.

Talk to me, dammit!

"Your husband is a very nice man, Ms. McCone," she said. "He was exhausted when he last looked in on you. You were asleep, so he left around nine, but told me to say he'd be back early tomorrow morning."

The nurse wiped my face with a tissue. "Don't cry. We're taking good care of you, and I understand that soon you will have a few visitors."

And I won't be able to smile at or talk with or hug any of them.

The tears kept coming.

"Don't cry," the nurse repeated. "Try to get some rest."

My emotions were running rampant. For a long time after the nurse left tears dribbled down my face. Self-pity morphed into fear and questions: Would I survive this? Would my life ever be the same?

What-ifs: What if I remained like this for the rest of my life? What if I was permanently confined to a wheelchair? Disabled in some other way? Couldn't fly our beautiful taildragger Cessna—Two-Seven-Tango? Couldn't ever hike on the cliffs at Touchstone? Or ride my horse, King Lear, at Hy's and my ranch?

The questions brought me to the edge of panic. The silent scream threatened to rise again, but I fought it off. Then, in its place, I felt a simmering of rage. How could this have happened to me? Who had shot me?

The lid came off the kettle of my emotions; rage reached full boil.

If I ever get out of this place, I'll hunt him down and kill him!

And I *would* get out of here. I'd reclaim my life. Nothing could stop me.

Yeah, right. Only paralysis and an inability to reach the world and the people I loved. . . .

More water leaked out of my eyes.

Damn roller coaster: self-pity, fear, panic, rage, determination, self-pity again. And I couldn't do a thing to control those feelings.

I couldn't control anything at all any more. . . .

Walking through the thick fog along the Embarcadero . . . The pier, empty and spooky . . . . On the catwalk, opening the door to my office . . . A sudden rushing motion, my head smacking into the wall.

And then the harsh fall onto the catwalk. Metal biting into my skin. The pop, the searing pain. Metal . . .

My eyes popped open, staring at the ceiling, which was dimly illuminated by a night-light.

Flashback to the night I'd been shot.

CRAIG MORLAND

The videos he'd taken from Harvey Davis's condo indicated a major sex scandal within city government—only he couldn't understand who was involved.

For once he was glad Adah wasn't home—some dinner with an old college friend that would probably go on long past midnight. He didn't want her to see any of this, not until he'd had time to evaluate it properly. The apartment did seem empty, though—a result of their elderly and obese cat, Charley, having died the previous winter. They planned to adopt another, but first Adah had been getting settled in with running the agency. Then they'd taken a series of weekend driving trips: to Carmel, Yountville, the Alexander Valley wine country. And his caseload had been heavy. Still, it was time. . . .

But not this weekend.

The doorbell rang. Craig moved on stockinged feet to the peephole and looked out. Mick. He'd called earlier and left a message on the machine that he'd concluded the Celestina Gates investigation and was now free to help on city hall. Craig went back into the living room, and after a few moments Mick's footsteps tapped away down the tiled steps.

It wasn't that Craig was jealously guarding his case or that he didn't find Mick a good investigator. But what he had planned was a delicate operation, and an additional person might attract attention. Since he'd worked for McCone, he'd become accustomed to going it on his own. Besides, what he planned to do was illegal and could compromise the agency.

God, he suddenly thought, maybe Mick had come here with bad news about Shar! He grabbed the phone and dialed the Brandt Institute. Ms. McCone was resting comfortably. No change.

He leaned back and thought about his boss. Initially there had been a veiled antipathy between them—typical fed-versus-cop-versus-private-investigator crap. And he hadn't liked it that she'd sensed his strong attraction to Adah early on and been highly protective of her friend. But then he'd moved to town and she'd immediately hired him, finally worked out the arrangement that kept him and Adah in San Francisco. Now, he knew, Shar was hoping the two of them would make it permanent, as she and Ripinsky had done.

Well, maybe they would, when Shar was well enough to attend. He was more than ready. Besides, it would be a hoot to introduce Adah's flaming liberal parents, Barbara and Rupert Joslyn, to his conservative WASP mother and father. Extremists, all four—and he suspected they'd get along famously, bonding in their shared disapproval of their children's lifestyles and career choices.

Enough. He needed to pack a bag and catch some sleep. By the time Adah returned from her women's night out he'd be on his way to Big Sur, where Supervisor Amanda Teller and State Representative Paul Janssen had scheduled their clandestine meeting.

MICK SAVAGE

He'd come to the Institute to commune with his aunt after Craig had pretended not to be home when he'd rung his doorbell. Did the former fed really think Mick didn't know he was there—or didn't he care? Either way, Mick had put his own fix on the situation.

Now he sat in the armchair in the quiet, dimly lighted room beside Shar's hospital bed, listening to the beep of the monitors. Hy hadn't been at the Institute when he'd arrived—exhausted, the nurse had said, and he'd finally gone home. She'd been kind enough to allow Mick some time with his aunt; it was an exclusive place and apparently didn't observe traditional visiting hours.

He'd been confined to a place like that last November, when he'd gotten drunk and stupid and thought he could somehow fly out of his misery on his Harley. But his injuries hadn't been life-threatening, and he'd been conscious, alert when he hadn't taken the strong pain meds—able to use his laptop to help Shar with a case she'd been working.

But Shar—her stillness frightened him. Her face, below the bandages on her head, was serene, unlined, as if she were many years younger. Maybe that was what was so unsettling: serenity wasn't Shar's thing. Keen concentration, purposefulness, action, yes. Laughter, tears, anger, and the occasional white-hot rage, too. But not this, never.

She'd always been his favorite aunt. He loved Aunt Patsy, but she was so flaky she made him nervous, and those three kids of hers, each by a different boyfriend—forget it. But Shar had been solid as a rock, taking him seriously, treating him like a man when he was only a kid.

Like when he'd pulled that stupid stunt of running away to San Francisco at Christmastime because his parents wouldn't give him a moped, and she'd found him and taken him home for Christmas dinner. Later, after his high school in Pacific Palisades had nailed him for hacking into their system and selling fellow students' confidential information, his folks had temporarily paroled him to Shar, and he'd ended up going to work for her permanently. When his mother had found another man and his dad had taken up with Rae, Shar had made him see that sometimes changes were for the best. And after the drunken Harley incident, she'd held his hand until the meds wiped the pain away.

He wondered if she was feeling any pain now.

Or maybe she was dreaming of something pleasant. Probably of flying the plane. Aside from being with Hy, he knew that was what she loved most, and more often than not they flew together.

Hy. The nurse had said he was exhausted. Not a word you usually associated with the man, but the emotional drain must be enormous. How long before it turned to rage and he did something violent? Hy had been a lot of things in his lifetime, and one of Shar's descriptions of him stuck in Mick's mind: *He's still dangerous.*

If anything would make Hy dangerous, it was this assault on Shar. What if he identified and went after the shooter by himself? The person was bound to be dangerous, too, could get the upper hand. Hy, streetwise and well trained as he was, still was not invincible.

Now Mick felt really scared. He couldn't bear to lose both of them.

HY RIPINSKY

I say we find the son of a bitch and just plain kill him. None of this justice-for-the-poor-misunderstood-criminal crap."

"You're drunk, John," Hy said, eyeing Sharon's tall, blond brother, who slumped in the armchair in their living room, beer bottle in hand.

"I'm not drunk, I'm pissed off. Aren't you?"

Hy sat down on the couch, set his own beer bottle on the end table. The sitting room of their restored earthquake cottage near the friendly, almost suburban—but recently crime-plagued—Glen Park district was small but comfortable. Light from the kiva-style fireplace gave the wooden wainscoting and pegged-pine floor a rosy glow.

He loved this house—even more than Touchstone or the ranch house that he'd inherited from his stepfather. Loved it because of the life they shared here on a regular basis. Allie, the calico cat, jumped onto his lap and pushed her nose at his hand for reassurance. Ralph, the orange tabby, crouched near the hearth, eyes watchful. Disruption like this affected animals as deeply as people, Hy thought, maybe more so because they couldn't understand what had gone wrong.

"So," John said belligerently, "are you or aren't you pissed off?"

"I'm more than pissed off," he replied. "Do I want to hunt the shooter down and kill him? Damn right. But at this point your sister needs me. Besides, the whole agency's on the case. They'll come up with something soon."

"And then they'll turn the info over to the cops, who'll arrest the prick. There'll be a trial. If Shar dies, maybe he'll get the death penalty but only after fifteen years of appeals—"

"She's *not* going to die."

They regarded each other silently.

"You've got to believe that," Hy added.

John's eyes went remote. Hy imagined what he was seeing: McCone as a little girl who resembled no one else in the family, supposedly a throwback to their Indian great-grandmother. McCone as an annoying preteen, always wanting to help him and their brother Joey with repairing their cars instead of playing with dolls the way she should. The high-school cheerleader; the first of them to go to college; the investigator who had reluctantly let her brother join in on a couple of cases. Hy knew much of this from Shar; he knew even more now because John had been waxing nostalgic—bordering on the maudlin—since he'd come up from San Diego and moved into their guest room nine days ago.

Frankly, he was sick of it.

To forestall any further reminiscences, he said, "Okay, say the folks at the agency identify the shooter and *don't* go to the police. What happens then?"

"We lure him to someplace where the body'll never be found and blow him away."

"Not so easy to do."

"What d'you mean? The whole California and Nevada desert is a boneyard. There're still people out there in Death Valley looking for the remains of Manson Family victims—and that happened over forty years ago, man."

"So how do you lure this guy to the desert?"

John frowned.

"Or do you kill him wherever he is and drive the body there—taking the chance you'll be involved in a traffic stop? How do you kill him? You don't know guns. A knife, strangulation? I've killed before, and it's not easy. In fact it's the hardest thing there is, even in self-defense. Just ask McCone—"

He realized what he'd said, put his hand over his eyes. Sweat began beading on his forehead and all at once he felt disoriented.

John stood and his big hand touched Hy's shoulder. "Hey, bro, I'll ask her as soon as I visit tomorrow. Even if she can't talk, she can answer me."

JULIA RAFAEL

The driveway was going on forever, and she couldn't see a thing. Didn't these people believe in lights?

The town of Sonoma had looked old-fashioned and pretty, with its central square and courthouse and restaurants and shops that had to be way out of most people's price range. Touristy— lots of people on the streets even at this hour. Couples holding hands; families eating ice cream cones. But the highway up the Valley of the Moon passed through a couple of rundown places full of shacks and old trailer parks, and then she was in the dark, wide-open country. She'd almost missed the secondary road that would take her to Peeples Winery. And now this . . .

She'd lived in the city too long to feel comfortable in the country. Had been born in Watsonville, but barely remembered Santa Cruz County or those artichoke fields her folks had worked—

What was that? A house lit up like a Christmas tree. *Dios*, it was huge—long and sprawling pale tan stucco with a second-story galleria and a steep tiled roof. Big old oak trees were illuminated by floodlights. No wonder the Peepleses had skimped on the driveway lighting: their PG&E bill must be thousands a month.

She pulled into the circular driveway, braked at the flagstone walk to the carved double front doors, then—suddenly ashamed of the car—moved it forward into the shadow of one of the oaks. She'd been so proud the day she bought the blue Toyota—her first car ever. Now it reminded her of how ordinary and marginal her life really was.

Well, maybe not so much any more. Things were going well. Next year, if she was careful about spending, she'd be able to send Tonio to a private school.

She went to the door and rang the bell. Soft, pretty chimes inside.

About half a minute later, Mrs. Peeples opened it. She was more frail than the last time Julia had seen her, and moving the heavy door seemed a strain. "Ms. Rafael," she said, her lined face tense, "thank you for coming."

"I'm glad to help."

"Please, come in."

She stepped into a long hallway running the length of the central wing of the house. When Judy Peeples struggled to shut the heavy door, Julia helped her. She noticed the tall, gray-haired woman was short of breath and took her arm to steady her. Mrs. Peeples smiled faintly and accepted her support.

"We'll go back to the den, where my husband's waiting," she said.

The den was at the rear of the house, past big, dark rooms opening off the hallway. Small and comfortable. Deep corduroy-covered chairs, faded and wrinkled from years of good use. Small color TV and a wall covered with bookshelves. Books also on the floor and end tables. The Peepleses matched the décor, both casually clad in jeans and T-shirts, Tom's ripped out at the knees. Tom was white-haired, tall and lean, with the kind of sun-browned face that told you he worked outside.

Judy Peeples had seemed on edge when she opened the door and now, in her husband's presence, even more so. Julia could feel the tension in the small room. Tom grunted a greeting and glared at his wife. Obviously Julia had interrupted a fight.

He said, "I told you to call her cellular and cancel."

"I couldn't do that, Tom."

"This is a reckless course. It could bring ruin to us, the winery, and Larry's memory."

"Of course Larry's memory comes last on the list."

Julia looked around and took a chair opposite where Judy Peeples stood in a defensive stance over her husband.

"You know," Mrs. Peeples said to him, "your objections aren't valid. We will survive. The winery will survive. But what we found in the tack room could be our only hope of learning what happened to our son. The only way of bringing him home to us."

How much cash *had* they found? And why was it in a tack room, of all places?

Julia said, "Mr. and Mrs. Peeples—"

They ignored her, turned up the volume of their argument.

"You're glad he's gone," Judy said. "He was always an embarrassment to you."

"How can you say that? I loved our son."

"Past tense."

"I *love* him."

"Nonsense. You've always looked down on him because you think he lacks intellect. And because he's gay."

"I think he lacks drive, not intelligence. As for him being gay, I have no prejudice in that area. Didn't I invite that Ben friend of his for weekends and holidays? Didn't I show him every courtesy? Don't I still, whenever he drops in?"

"A butler would behave more warmly than you do."

"Please listen to me," Julia said.

Neither of them looked her way.

"Goddamn it, Judy, what do you want from me?"

"What do I want? I want my son back!" Judy Peeples bent forward from the waist, hugging her midriff, and began to cry. "This may be our last opportunity—no matter what he's done—to find him and bring him home."

Tom Peeples's lined face crumpled and he put his hand over his eyes, but he made no effort to comfort his wife.

At last Julia could step into the situation. She went over, put her arms around Judy Peeples's bent body, and helped her into a chair.

After a moment, Tom Peeples stood, his lined face resigned, and laid a rough hand on his wife's shoulder. "You're right," he said. "It's just so hard for me to accept it."

She looked up at him, eyes streaming.

"I'll do anything you ask, if it'll bring Larry back to us."

". . . Thank you, Tom."

To Julia, Peeples added, "Please excuse our quarreling. We're not ourselves today. Haven't been in six months, actually."

"No problem. You've been dealing with stuff I can't even imagine. Will you show me the money now?"

"Yes. Come with me, please."

He led her into the hallway, through an informal dining room and a kitchen that Julia would have killed for. All this money, she thought, all this land, but these people were broken. The loss of an only child, the uncertainty of what had happened to him—that made every material thing meaningless.

If Tonio vanished without a trace, she would spend her life searching—and grieving.

Peeples led her along a lighted graveled path through an oak grove.

"My wife thinks this money will lead you to some magical solution to our son's disappearance."

"But you don't."

"No. I'm not doubting your abilities, but I think if Larry disappeared voluntarily he's hidden himself where no one can find him. Or else . . ."

"Yes?"

"Foul play." Peeples's voice was choked.

Hombre pobricito. He couldn't bring himself to use the word *dead.*

They came to a big white barn. When Peeples opened its doors, the smell took Julia aback, and she hesitated.

"You afraid of horses?" Peeples asked. "They're all confined to their stalls. They'll get restless when we go in, but settle down pretty quick."

"I don't know anything about horses," she told him, "but the smell . . ."

"Well, yes, they're stinky buggers. I'm not crazy about them myself, but my wife, she loves them. We've got six. She gives free riding lessons to the vineyard workers' kids."

Julia started liking the Peepleses a lot more.

Peeples turned on a light. At first it blinded Julia, then she started, face-to-face with a blond horse that had a white star on its forehead. It whinnied, but its brown eyes were gentle.

"This way," Peeples said.

The tack room was to the right. It was small, with saddles on stands, its walls covered with riding apparatus, none of which Julia could identify. Until tonight she hadn't been any closer to a horse than the ones the police rode in the city parks.

Peeples said, "I was moving some things around in here this afternoon, trying to consolidate them. There was a loose floorboard under one box that I'd never noticed before." He went to the far side, pried up the board, and lifted out a small leather travel bag.

"One hundred thousand dollars," he said in a hollow voice. "Small bills. I've counted it twice."

He held out the bag and Julia looked into it. Rows of bills banded together. More money than she'd ever seen in one place.

Peeples looked down at her, his tanned face slack and aged beyond his fifty-some years.

"I can't believe our son stole this money and hid it here," he said. "But how else could he have gotten his hands on this much cash?"

Right, Julia thought, *how else?*

"Do you have a safe?" she asked.

"Yes."

"Then let's put it there until I figure out what to do about this."

SATURDAY, JULY 19

JULIA RAFAEL

The late supper Judy Peeples had promised her had been good, their guest room was super-comfortable, but it was too damn quiet in the country. She could sleep through the wail of sirens and the grumbling of buses and people shouting on the city streets, but here in rural Sonoma County, where the only sound was a rooster that kept crowing all night, she tossed and turned. Weren't roosters supposed to crow only at dawn? What was *wrong* with the thing?

Around three in the morning she got up and sat on the window seat looking out at the oak grove between the house and the stables. She focused on the slight movement of the branches in the breeze, and after a while she felt sleepy. The bird had finally shut up. Maybe she could—

Motion under the oak trees.

Julia tensed up. An animal? What wild kinds did they have here? Deer, raccoons, opossums. For all she knew, coyotes and mountain lions. Well, she was safe inside. . . .

But this shape didn't move like an animal, it moved like a human. Larry or Judy Peeples, going to check on the horses? No, she'd have seen them or heard the back door close if they'd left the house.

The dark figure kept moving. In the direction of the stables?

She got up quickly, pulled on jeans, and tucked her sleep shirt into them. Went out into the hall. A night-light burned there, showing her the way to the stairs. She crept down them, guided by another light on the first floor, then felt her way back to the door off the kitchen.

The night air was warm and felt like silk against her skin. Something tickled her nostrils, and she had to stifle a sneeze. From her second-floor bedroom the night hadn't seemed so dark because of a scattering of stars, but out here it was inky. She started toward the oak grove, and the damn rooster went off again. Nearly made her jump a foot.

She moved through the grove, keeping to the path, wishing she'd thought to put on shoes.

Estúpida. When will you learn?

The stones cut into her soles; a couple of times she had to hop on one foot. Finally the stables came into view. Dark, but the horses sounded restless.

So here she was—barefoot and unarmed. Unarmed because after all the violence she'd seen growing up on the streets of the Mission district, she hated guns and had opted out of getting firearms-qualified. And suddenly scared. What had she been thinking of, coming out here like this?

Movement by the stables—slow, stealthy. A bulky shape slipping off to the left. Unarmed or not, Julia took off running in pursuit.

The person—she couldn't tell if it was a man or a woman— plunged into the vineyard that bordered the stables, heading toward the road. Feet pounded the dirt between the plants, branches snapped and rustled. Julia followed through the rows of gnarled old vines.

After a moment she stopped to get her bearings. The person she was following must've stopped too: there was no noise except for the distant cry of the rooster. Then another bird joined the chorus. No one moved among the vines.

Julia wiped beads of sweat from her forehead, looked around. Blackness, crouching shadows. Narrow paths stretching in all directions. Then, off to her left, a faint rustling. The intruder was on the move again.

She went toward the sound, took a path, and ran down it, kick-

ing up clods of dirt. The intruder's footsteps now sounded uneven, labored.

Julia was gaining, gaining—

Then in the darkness something slammed into her. An up-
right grape stake. Pain erupted on the bridge of her nose, and
she fell to the ground, the gnarled vines scratching on her way
down. She lay there stunned for a few seconds. By the time she
regained her senses and her feet, a car's engine had started up in
the distance.

Lost them, whoever he—or she—was.

Mierda.

She put her hand to her nose, felt blood welling. Injury to in-
sult. This was a great beginning to her day.

SHARON McCONE

*P*ale pinkish light seeping around the drawn blinds. Must be very early in the morning. There's been a shift in the weather, I can feel it. Today will be beautiful.

But not for me.

I lay there, depression gathering again. After the nightmare flashback to when I'd been shot, I'd had a peculiar dream in which Hy was looking into my eyes, but he couldn't speak any more than I could. Then others appeared—Mick, Rae, Ted, Ma—and they couldn't speak either. And finally I realized it wasn't that they couldn't—they wouldn't. Keeping something from me.

I thought back to Hy's behavior the day before. At first he'd been elated to connect with me. Then they'd done a CT scan and some other tests, and he was a little subdued but still upbeat. But later he'd been quiet, wrapped up in his own thoughts, and his smile was slightly off.

Definitely holding something back. Something those tests had revealed.

Dammit, if that was the case, I deserved to know. When he came in today, I'd ask him—

Right. I couldn't ask him anything. All I could do was respond to questions.

All I could do was lie here. Silent. Motionless. Afraid.

CRAIG MORLAND

The sky was glowing over the eastern hills when he awoke, cramped and cold, in his SUV at a pullout on Highway 1 near Big Sur. He'd driven almost to the Spindrift Lodge, where San Francisco's president of the board of supervisors and the state representative had arranged their secret meeting, then parked about ten miles north. No reason to arrive in the middle of the night and roust the innkeeper from his or her bed; no need to attract attention to himself. Amanda Teller and Paul Janssen would probably check in in the afternoon, and by then he'd be tucked away, hopefully in an adjoining unit.

He ran his hands over his face and hair, then got out of the car and breathed in the crisp salt air. Fog misted the gray sea; its waves smacked onto the rocks some thousand feet below. But the pink light to the east indicated the day would clear. He turned that way and looked up: towering pine-covered slopes, through which a waterfall had cut a channel. Now, because of the dry summer conditions inland, its flow was barely a trickle. Come the rainy season, it would be a torrent.

All around there were reminders of the 2008 wildfire, sparked by lightning, that had burned more than 160,000 acres in the area: blackened sections, redwoods with charred branches, deadfalls. Many residents had lost their homes, even more had been evacuated, and the Pacific Coast Highway had been closed to traffic. People in the Big Sur area were strong and resilient, though; it had always been subject to floods, mudslides, and avalanches. Often in winter it was cut off from the surrounding territory, but no matter how bad the disaster the community clung together and regrouped quickly.

Craig loved Big Sur, but he and Adah had spent little time there. It was remote, down a very dicey part of the coast highway, and there really wasn't much to do. Better to go to Carmel, with its interesting shops and good restaurants, for a getaway. Still, there was something magical about this long stretch of tall trees and rugged sea cliffs; if he were a believer, he'd say being here was akin to a religious experience.

But he wasn't a believer. His exposure to religion had been limited to Christmas Eve and Easter services at the Methodist church in Alexandria, Virginia, where he'd been raised. He never contemplated the existence of a deity or eternal life; it simply wasn't in his makeup. Adah was the same: she'd been reared in the religion of her parents—communism—but she hadn't taken her radical parents' beliefs too seriously. In fact, when they'd become disillusioned and begun labeling themselves as "wild-eyed liberals," she'd been relieved.

He thought of Shar: what did she believe? She'd been raised Catholic, but he'd never known her to go to church. And the beliefs of her Indian ancestors hadn't been passed on to her. He hoped if she had any faith at all she was leaning heavily on it now, during the toughest battle of her life.

Nature called. He went into a stand of pines clinging to the clifftop, out of eyeshot of early passing motorists. Returning, he looked at his watch. Six-thirty. He'd grab breakfast somewhere, even if it meant driving north, then play tourist till around ten, a respectable time to arrive at the Spindrift Lodge for a spontaneous weekend getaway.

RAE KELLEHER

She was starting her search for Bill Delaney, the name she'd found in the phone book in Callie O'Leary's hotel room, when the fog showed signs of breaking over the Golden Gate. Delaney's cellular had been out of service consistently when she'd called it last night during breaks in a family evening with Ricky and the girls.

She was surprised how much she enjoyed the times when Molly and Lisa, their older sister Jamie, and even their troubled brother Brian were in residence. The eldest girl, Chris, was a student at Berkeley and dropped in often. So did Mick.

Family had never played a big part in Rae's life—unless you counted the people at All Souls and, later, at the agency. Her parents had died in an accident when she was just a kid, and she'd been raised by her grandmother in Santa Maria—a cold, begrudging woman who had died of a heart attack while trying to murder a perfectly good rosebush.

Maybe that was why she could put up with the trials and tribulations of the Little Savages: they were so much more of a family than Nana, as the old lady had insisted Rae call her.

Of course, there was Jamie's abortion last year: Rae had finessed that so Ricky hadn't made it more stressful than was warranted upon his second daughter. And while Brian's OCD, which had surfaced shortly before Charlene and Ricky divorced, was difficult to deal with, he was a sweet-natured boy and lately Rae had become close to him. Brian seemed better all the time; he did get manic once in a while, dusting and washing everything in sight, but Rae kind of appeciated that. In spite of their having a full-time housekeeper and a maid, chores at the Kelleher-Savage home were often left undone, what with the band members and recording company people and friends constantly traipsing through the house.

Back to the search for Bill Delaney. She'd called his cellular minutes ago. Same lack of response. No way of knowing whether it was Callie who'd written down the number or when. The phone could've been a throwaway or the account canceled long ago. With no information on Delaney, an ordinary name in this city with its high Irish population, locating him wouldn't be easy.

Okay, if a hooker had his cell number, what could he be?

A fellow sex worker. A pimp. Someone in the porn industry. A lawyer . . .

Yes!

Google search of ABA members. Many Delaneys. She worked her way through them, both in the city and around the state. Narrowed it down by type of law practice. Came up with two possibles, one on Forty-eighth Avenue near Ocean Beach, the other on Shotwell Street, close to where the former All Souls Victorian stood on Bernal Heights. It was Saturday, but ambulance chasers who bailed hookers out of jail were always reachable.

As she passed through the living room on the way out, she called to Ricky, Molly, and Lisa, "When you go to the zoo, tell the baby giraffe hello for me."

Ricky had an arm around either daughter. They were watching something on TV that sounded nonsensical. He grinned and said, "Good hunting, Red."

HY RIPINSKY

"She has got to be told today, before the visitors start coming," he said to Dr. Saxnay.

The older man sighed. "You're right, of course. We'll give her the weekend to take it in, then allow the first visitors on Monday."

"I'd rather they start coming right away."

"The diagnosis is going to be a shock."

"She's aware it's bad. All that time when she could hear and no one knew it. Besides, with Sharon, even knowing the worst is better than uncertainty."

Ralph Saxnay said, "Well, you can attest to that better than I." He got up from the desk and led Hy toward McCone's room. "You go in first."

It was an attractive room—he hadn't paid attention to that before—with pale blue walls and matching blue upholstery on the visitors' armchair near the high hospital bed. None of this backache-making plastic hospital-room stuff that he could swear was designed to drive family and friends away. Today the room was fragrant, filled with the flowers and plants from well-wishers that had arrived steadily since word got out that she'd been admitted here. The blinds were raised, giving a view of the silver-leafed eucalyptus grove, and the nursing staff had apparently completed their morning routine.

Shar was awake, propped against the pillows. He went to her, kissed lips that were moist with Chap Stick. Looked into her eyes.

She was blinking frantically.

Yeah, she knows something's wrong. And she wants me to tell her what.

Saxnay had come up behind him. He seemed to intuit what was going on.

"I've come to talk with you about your CT scan results," he began, moving to where Sharon could see him.

McCone blinked once.

"Frankly, they are not as good as we'd hoped. Now that we know you're conscious and aware, we can put a name to your condition: locked-in syndrome."

The doctor proceeded to explain: the same litany of symptoms and causes Hy had been given: awareness, ability to reason, to feel emotion and touch. Saxnay didn't downplay the seriousness of the prognosis, and throughout his speech, McCone's gaze remained fixed and unblinking on the doctor's.

"I don't mean to say your condition is hopeless," Saxnay concluded. "Patients have made partial recoveries. Much depends on you—your spirit, your determination. And, of course, you have friends and family to rally round you. That means a lot." He paused. "Have I explained clearly enough for now?"

McCone blinked once.

"Then I'll leave you two alone."

"Thank you, Doctor," Hy said, and pulled the upholstered chair close to the bed.

A single tear slipped down his wife's right cheek. Gently he wiped it away, then did the same with one that appeared on her left cheek. He touched her arm, wished he could take her hand, but it was under the covers, stuck with an IV.

"This isn't as bad as he made it sound," he said.

No blink or eye movement.

"We'll get through it."

No response.

"Doctors don't know everything."

Eye movement—questioning the statement, he thought.

"Would you like me to go? Be alone for a while?"

Two blinks.

"Then I'll stay and tell you what the folks at the agency are doing to ID whoever did this to you."

SHARON McCONE

A *vegetable. A fucking vegetable.*
I remember when I was younger, laughing at people with *disabilities, the horrible words we used: feeb, spaz, veg.*

Well, join the club. For the rest of your life, somebody somewhere'll *be laughing at you.*

Tears slipped down my cheeks again. God, I hadn't cried this much in my life!

Actually, what I felt like when the doctor was talking to me was a lab rat in a cage. Saxnay seemed like a good surgeon, but in my case he didn't have much to work with and he knew it.

A lab rat. No, that wasn't right. Lab rats could move, make sounds, eat on their own. I was more like a mummy. I liked that term better than the *veg* word.

The effort the agency people were putting into my case touched me, though. At least I was a cherished mummy. Hy said they'd be coming by and starting to report to me tomorrow; relatives would arrive, too.

Ma . . . At first I'd thought, Jesus Christ, not Ma on the first day! But Hy had said he'd arrange for the RI jet to pick her up in San Diego tomorrow afternoon; he'd take her to dinner and put her up at an expensive boutique hotel downtown that she liked. The former Katie McCone had become used to her creature comforts since she'd remarried and become Kay Hunt, but she still had a good heart and I loved her. It was just the drama I couldn't take.

Rae and Ricky, John, Charlene and Vic. Mick, Ted, Julia, Craig, Adah. And everybody else. God I missed them!

I'm starting to look forward to something. . . .

This case. That was what I was particularly looking forward to. Hearing the details of how they'd go about finding the bastard who'd altered my life—maybe irrevocably.

But could they do it without me? I thought about that for a while. Something light rose in my chest, like a shiny bubble, and I would have smiled if that had been possible.

You've heard of an armchair detective, folks? How about a locked-in investigator?

JULIA RAFAEL

She took the exit from the Bay Bridge and drove toward the pier, fussing over whether she'd done the right thing to leave the money in the Peepleses' safe and agree not to report it to the authorities. Wished she could ask Shar about it. Of course Shar—who claimed to be a by-the-book investigator—probably would've said it was wrong. But then Shar's own actions didn't always follow what the book said.

She'd left the vineyard early, leaving a thank-you note and creeping out into the predawn light before the Peepleses stirred. She didn't want to explain her injury or tell them that someone—maybe their missing son—had been sneaking around the stables, probably trying to retrieve the cash; the news would only increase their anguish, and Julia doubted the person would return.

Her nose hurt and she had a bloody scab, partially concealed by makeup. She wouldn't be surprised if her eyes were blackened within a few hours. She'd taken punches to the nose before, and that was the inevitable result.

Julia parked in her slot on the pier's floor and hurried up the stairs to the catwalk. Half an hour late for the staff meeting, and she felt like shit. She rushed into the conference room. Stopped. Where was everybody?

Back down the catwalk to Ted's office. He and Patrick Neilan were there, Ted sitting in his chair, Patrick perched on a corner of the desk. Ted's bright red Western-style shirt—the latest of his

ever-changing fashion statements—contrasted sharply with Patrick's goth black.

"Is the meeting over?" she asked.

"Never got started," Patrick said. "Adah and Derek and Thelia
showed, but none of the folks who are actively working the case.
Hy—who requested the meeting—was on time, but left when we
realized it wasn't going to happen."

"Craig wasn't home when Adah got there last night," Ted added,
"and there's been no word from him. Mick's cellular is out of service range. Ricky said Rae went out in a hurry around ten. What
the hell happened to you?"

"Hostile encounter with a grape stake." She explained about
her visit to the Peepleses. "Did I do right, leaving the money
there?"

Patrick shrugged, running a hand through his spiky red hair.

Ted said, "It's what Shar would've done."

"So what do we do now?" she asked.

"Other than you icing your face? I'll keep calling around," Ted
told her. "Maybe I can gather the troops this afternoon. In the
meantime, Shar's entertaining visitors."

Julia entered Shar's room hesitantly, an ice bag that the
nurse on the desk had provided pressed to her nose. It would
help to keep her eyes from blackening, the woman said. Ice
hadn't done anything for her in the past, but she accepted the
bag gratefully.

Shar was turned on her side before a window overlooking a
eucalyptus grove. The room was quiet and fragrant with flowers.
Julia skirted the bed, drew up the single chair, and looked into
Shar's eyes.

Light filled them, and Shar blinked.

"You're awake," Julia said.

Another blink.

Dios, it was creepy! She'd never seen Shar so motionless and
silent. How the hell did they know she was in there anyway? This
blinking could be a reflex.

No. Ted had said she was completely aware, that one blink meant yes and two meant no.

Still, it *was* creepy.

A questioning light came into Shar's eyes. She stared steadily at Julia's ice bag.

"Oh, this," Julia said, "*de nada*. I'll explain."

She gave Shar a full report on her cases. Asked the same thing she'd asked herself, Ted, and Patrick. "Did I do the right thing leaving the money with the Peepleses?"

One blink. Yes.

"What should I do now? Oh, hell, I know you can't answer me. But I just don't . . ."

Shar's gaze fixed on hers, strong and compelling.

"Okay, I could turn it over to the police."

Two blinks. *No.*

"Right. We're not even sure it's stolen."

Blink.

"But I don't think this guy who worked in the stockroom at Home Showcase saved that much out of his salary. Or won the lottery. And if he had, it'd be earning interest in a bank, rather than stuffed in a duffel bag under the floorboards of his parents' tack room."

Blink.

"We don't even know he's the one who put it there. Right?"

Blink.

"Or if he was the one I chased through the vineyard?"

Blink.

"So what do I . . . ? Dig deeper, way deeper into the guy's life?"

Blink. Then Shar closed her eyes. Tired.

Julia sat by the bed a few minutes more before leaving quietly only when she was sure Shar was asleep.

MICK SAVAGE

God, these tracking devices were getting better and better!

He sat on his Harley—a more powerful version of the one he'd wrecked last fall—across from the Spindrift Lodge near Big Sur. The lodge was old and sprawling, its logs washed silver-gray by the elements. Woodstove chimneys protruded above each unit, and the ice plant lawn between the semicircular driveway was strewn with driftwood. Craig had just checked in—unit twenty. Mick wasn't about to go up and knock on the door, though; he'd wait it out, see what happened.

Last night after he left Craig and Adah's apartment he'd located Craig's SUV where it was parked a block away and slapped a tracking device under the bumper. At three in the morning Mick's monitor showed the vehicle was in motion. Mick left his condo and followed.

Why, he wondered on the long drive down, was Craig being so damn secretive about his line of investigation? Sure, it was politically sensitive, but it might have something to do with Shar getting shot and paralyzed. Well, maybe it was just the old FBI training kicking in. Or maybe Craig wanted to score a big one for himself.

No, Craig wasn't like that. What he was looking into had to be something major. And he wanted to be sure of his facts before he enlisted the rest of them.

An hour passed. The sky was clear, but a cold wind was blow-ing in and the sea was beating against the cliffs, throwing up big fans of spray. Good weather in Big Sur didn't last long.

As he waited and watched, Mick thought back to the night last November when he'd been on a similar stretch of highway, drunk out of his mind and stoned on grief because he'd lost the woman he'd considered the love of his life, Charlotte Keim. So drunk and stoned he'd decided to see how high the Harley could fly above the Pacific. He'd misjudged and landed hard on the roadside, hard enough to injure himself seriously and knock some sense into him. Sweet Charlotte had done the same: she was seven years older than he, and during repeated conversations over the next couple of months she'd convinced him that life and love didn't end at twenty-two.

She was getting married next month to an old college sweetheart. He wished her well.

Activity at the inn. A car—plain, gray, probably a rental—pulled in. A woman in jeans and a dark-colored jacket, her head covered with a scarf, got out and went into the office. She returned quickly, retrieved a bag from the car, and entered Room 19, next to Craig's.

Mick took out his binoculars, noted the license plate of the car. Jotted down her time of arrival.

Half an hour later another inconspicuous sedan arrived. White this time. A man in jeans and a parka, its hood pulled up and resting low on his brow, got out and went to register. When he came out, he moved the car and entered Room 21, to the other side of Craig. Mick noted down the plate number and time.

For an hour after that, nothing happened. It was getting cold on the clifftop: icy gusts of wind ruffled his hair and permeated his leather jacket. Finally he started the Harley and drove into the inn's parking lot. The pleasant woman at the desk agreed to give him Room 22.

"That's the second request I've had today for a certain room number," she said. "Man came in this morning and took Room Twenty, said he was meeting two associates; he described them and asked they be put on either side of him. Said not to mention he was here—it was a surprise. You a member of his party, too?"

"Yes, ma'am, I am." He wanted to ask her the names all three had registered under, but didn't want to arouse her suspicions. "Any good takeout places that deliver around here?"

"There's a pizza joint, but I wouldn't recommended it." There was an ominous tone to her voice.

Mick was glad he always carried a couple of nutrition bars. It could be a long night.

RAE KELLEHER

The second of the Bill Delaneys turned out to be Callie O'Leary's attorney. He had his office in the front room of his shabby Victorian on Shotwell Street in Bernal Heights, two blocks from All Souls' former headquarters. When Rae came to his door and said she was an investigator hired to locate Callie so she could claim an inheritance left her by her grandmother, Delaney let her in, but the small eyes that peered out of poochy folds of flesh were shrewd and wary.

He probably didn't believe her but hoped there might be something in it for him.

Delaney urged her to take one of his clients' chairs and sat behind his old oak desk. The room's sagging shelves were lined with law books, but the bindings looked brittle and were faded by the sun coming through the unshaded bay window. The air smelled of dust and stale cigar smoke; the collar and cuffs of Delaney's blue oxford cloth shirt were frayed. Rae felt much better dressed in her jeans and sweater.

"So Ms. O'Leary is an heiress," Delaney said, folding his stubby-fingered hands on a file in front of him.

"I wouldn't put it that way, but the sum is substantial for a . . . woman of her means."

"And how would you know about Ms. O'Leary's 'means'?"

"I've been to her last address. And from what people tell me, she was a hooker."

Delaney frowned reprovingly. "A sex worker, Ms. Kelleher. There's a difference."

She ignored his correction. "Can you provide me with Ms. O'Leary's present address?"

"She doesn't wish it to be made known. She calls me periodically, however. Perhaps you could leave the check for the inheritance with me, and I'll hold it for her."

Right. Did she look like she had an IQ of twenty?

"Sorry, no. First she'll have to sign some documents in the presence of a notary."

"Then I can't help you, Ms. Kelleher."

"Will you at least pass on a message asking her to call me?" Rae extended one of her cards.

"Certainly." He took it, tossed it carelessly on the desk, and stood up. "More than anything else, I'd like to see my client financially secure and out of her present dubious occupation."

Sure he would. But only if she'd go halves with him.

When she got back to her car—a lovely black BMW Z4 that Ricky had given her on her birthday two years ago—Rae checked her cell phone for messages. One from Ted, asking why the hell she'd missed the staff meeting, and another from Maggie Lambert of Victims' Advocates. She wanted a report.

The Advocates had their offices only a few blocks away on Valencia Street. Rae decided she might as well go there and talk with Lambert in person.

The offices were up a dimly lighted, mildewy-smelling staircase above a taqueria. While many blocks of Valencia Street were now lined with good restaurants and chichi shops, the economic upturn hadn't reached this pocket of poverty. At the top Rae pushed through the door and entered a room full of cast-off furnishings. Maggie Lambert—short, gray-haired, and clad in faded jeans and a red flannel shirt with one button missing—sat at her desk leafing through a thick file. When she looked up and saw Rae, her face became stern.

"Rae, thank you for coming. Is there any progress in the Angie Atkins case?"

Trust Maggie to get right to the point. Rae said, "I've got a lead to that friend of hers I told you about—Callie O'Leary."

"And that's it?"

"Her attorney will put us in touch when he hears from her."

"This is very unsatisfactory."

Rae bit back a tart retort about asking a lot of someone who was working pro bono. Said, "I'm not happy with it myself. If I could talk with Callie, she might be able to tell me more about Angie. From the police report, I gather that's not her true identity, but there's no guarantee she told Callie anything other than her street name."

"What about dental records? DNA? Did you ask the police about them?"

Maggie must've been watching too many episodes of *CSI*. "In order to compare dental charts, you need to have some idea of who the victim was. DNA samples were taken and stored, but they didn't match any in the current databases."

"So exactly what is it you intend to do?"

"Wait for Callie O'Leary's attorney to call. Talk with the investigating officers at the SFPD again. Comb through my files for overlooked leads. Especially anything that may connect this case with my employer's shooting."

Maggie's face softened. "How's she doing?"

"As well as can be expected. In fact, I'm going to visit her now: even though she can't speak, I suspect she'll be a great source of inspiration."

SHARON McCONE

I closed my eyes after Rae left my room. Even with brief naps I was exhausted. Besides Hy and her, I'd had three other visitors: Julia, my sister Charlene, and my brother John. Enough already.

I was beginning to understand the routine of this place. The sun was slanting low on the eucalyptus grove, which meant the nurse would soon come in, check my vital signs, catheter, and feeding tube, and turn me onto my other side. I'd doze, and when I woke Hy would be there. He'd leave late, and then there'd be another visit from the nurse. If I was lucky, I'd sleep deeply for a few hours. If not, I'd face my demons alone in the dark.

My demons were large and numerous: looming figures from the past, including the dark one who had shot me. Vague shadows of the future—fleeting, unreal, frightening. And my present . . .

Good God, is this *going to be my life?*

No. No way I could face that.

So what's your alternative? Suicide?

I'd always considered suicides to be cowards, heedless of the damage they did to those who loved them. Leaving messes behind for others to clean up, as my brother Joey had done when he'd overdosed on booze and drugs in a lumber-town shack outside of Eureka. On one level I hated Joey for the pain he'd inflicted on my family members and me—particularly for causing the shadows that, even on a happy day, never left my mother's eyes. But Joey had been facing demons he apparently couldn't control; now, facing my own, I began to wonder if he hadn't done us, as well as himself, a favor.

And if I were to remain in this state indefinitely? No way I could endure that. I'd rather just check out.

But California didn't have an assisted-suicide law. And asking assistance from someone I loved—namely Hy—would put a terrible burden on him.

Besides, I wanted to live. I'd reached a point in my life where I could say I was happy and looking forward to a good future. At least I had been, until someone fired a bullet into my skull.

I felt the rage bubble and boil over again. I wished I could scream invectives, hit something, smash the vase of roses placed prominently within my range of vision.

Slowly I regained control. Calm and purpose returned. I would not die a suicide, even if it was possible, because that would be giving in to the scumbag who shot me.

I began going over everything I'd been told so far, hunting for a lead that might ID him.

Slow, soft footsteps creeping toward me. Then a noisy rush.
Flash of light. Pain, pain, pain.
Chains pulling at me.
I wasn't dreaming; it was another hideous, very real flashback.

HY RIPINSKY

He waited under the shelter of the Cessna's high wing, in his tie-down space at Oakland Airport's North Field. The afternoon was clear but windy—windy enough to make the wings of the neighboring aircraft, a homebuilt, creak and groan. After a while a man cut through the rows of planes and approached him: near six feet five, heavily muscled, wearing a brown leather flight jacket as battered as Hy's own and a plain blue baseball cap pulled low on his forehead.

Len Weathers, an acquaintance from the old days in Bangkok. Weathers kept a Cessna Citation here at the field, and Hy and he had exchanged nods over the years, but they'd never spoken. Neither wanted to acknowledge those old days, and Hy didn't want to acknowledge Weathers because of what it was rumored he'd become.

The word was that Weathers freelanced as an enforcer for various unsavory elements in California and Nevada. Among his alleged services were kidnapping and murder for hire. The same forces that had operated in Southeast Asia during the post-Vietnam era—greed, ruthlessness, and preying upon the weak and helpless—had affected both him and Hy in vastly different ways. Hy had returned with a load of guilt and nightmares enough to last his lifetime and—in time—a desire to make the world a better place. Weathers had continued in an ugly, downward spiral.

Hy had been certain he'd never again exchange a word with Len Weathers. But now he needed one of the man's services.

Weathers ducked under the wing. Shook Hy's hand. Said, "I understand you've got a problem."

Hy had relayed his desire to talk with Weathers through one of the line men at the fuel pumps.

"Yeah," he replied. "My wife—"

"I know what happened to your wife."

"Her agency and I are working on finding whoever did it."

"How does that concern me?"

"It doesn't until we find the person."

Their eyes met and held, each man taking the other's measure. Hy flashed back to Bangkok: Weathers had been a hotdog pilot for K-Air, the flight service Hy was employed by, and a tough man. But there'd been a good-natured, humorous side to him. Now there was no trace of that; he was cold and hard and exuded the scent of danger.

Weathers also had not aged well; although he was only in his forties, his face was deeply lined. A scar from a knife fight in Bangkok cut crazily across his forehead, and Hy had noticed a limp as he approached. A few more years and he'd look like an old man.

What happened to you, Weathers? What happened to me *that I'd be standing here about to ask you to do this thing?*

Well, he knew what had happened to him. McCone had been shot and might die.

"Okay," Weathers said after a moment. "You want me to take him or her out?"

"No."

"Why not?"

"Because this person is mine. But I want to know if I can call on you if there's a problem."

"Call on me any time you want. I've got to warn you—I don't come cheap."

"I don't care about price; it's dependability I'm after."

"Deal." Weathers held out his hand.

Hy took it, thinking, My God, I feel as if I'm shaking hands with the Devil.

CRAIG MORLAND

He'd spent the afternoon replaying the videos he'd taken from Harvey Davis's condo. Young women and major players in state and city politics, engaging in all sorts of explicit sex acts. No clue as to who the women were—save one—but surprise and outright shock about the male participants. By the time the doors opened and closed in the rooms to either side of him, he felt both grim and outraged. Dirty all over again.

He picked up the earpieces to the listening devices he'd earlier installed.

Supervisor Amanda Teller sighed, unzipped her travel bag, and ran a bath.

Representative Paul Janssen went out for ice, opened a bottle and poured into what sounded like one of the plastic glasses provided in the bathroom. A chair groaned.

Teller bathed. Janssen drank. Craig fiddled with the volume on the earpieces and their connections to his recorders.

The phone rang in Janssen's room. "Yeah," he said. "I'll be right there."

Noises from Janssen's room; his door closed and his footsteps went toward Teller's unit. He tapped on the door, and seconds later was admitted.

"Good trip down?" she asked.

"As if you care."

"No need to be hostile in these beautiful surroundings."

"Why not? Did you hear about Harvey Davis being killed?"

"Yes. Poor man."

"That's all you can say? Don't you understand what his murder means to you and me?"

"Suppose you spell it out."

"Harvey knew, or maybe only suspected, what was going on. But he was an insatiable information gatherer; the reason he was shot is that they knew he had those videos. If they know you've figured it out—"

"Don't be nonsensical, Paul. I didn't tell Harvey anything he didn't need to know." Teller paused, and there was a rustling of papers. "I have the document right here. I'll go over it with you."

"I'm perfectly able to read legal documents by myself."

"Whatever."

Silence. Pages being turned.

"This clause—it's vaguely worded." Janssen.

"Let me see. . . . Oh, yes, of course. Go ahead and insert clearer wording and initial it."

"All right—you bitch."

"Paul, do you have to be so unpleasant? Let's have a drink—I have a bottle of good single malt."

"I wouldn't drink with you—"

"But you used to."

"Much to my disadvantage."

"You should learn to hold your liquor a lot better."

"There are many things I should learn. You too, Amanda."

"Meaning?"

"You think you've pulled off a big coup, but these people are dangerous. Consider what they did to Harvey."

"You're an alarmist, my dear. The document will remain safe with me, so long as you hold up your end of the bargain. Speaking of that . . . ?"

"The transfer will take place Monday morning."

"Good. Now sign the document."

"Gladly. It may be your death warrant."

"You know, Paul, you really ought to get some help for your

paranoia. It's beginning to cloud your judgment and make you unpleasant to deal with."

"I ought to tear this up and shove it up your ass!"

"Just sign it."

A long pause and then, "Done."

"How about that drink now?"

"I'd sooner drink with Hitler."

"Whatever."

A chair moved. Footsteps went toward the unit's door.

Teller said, "In spite of your insults and acid tone, it's been a pleasure."

"Go to hell!"

Door opening and closing. Janssen returning to his room.

Teller was silent. Then Craig heard her laughing softly.

Something thudded into the wall between Janssen's unit and his.

"Filthy bitch! Cunt! I hope to God you get yours!"

In her room, Teller was pouring a drink. Then she called a pizza delivery service. No sound except ice clinking and liquor pouring from either unit until the pizza arrived. Then Janssen's room went totally silent, and Teller switched on the TV to a cop drama. Craig ate the deli sandwich he'd brought with him, continued to monitor both rooms, and when the TV went off in Teller's, he went to bed with the earpieces on.

He'd been up since seven on Friday morning, and he sank immediately into a deep sleep.

SUNDAY, JULY 20

MICK SAVAGE

It was after midnight, but he couldn't sleep. He wished he'd brought along a good book. TV was miserable at this hour.

He'd followed Craig to Big Sur on an impulse, and now he considered the foolishness of it. If Craig found out, he'd be pissed and probably never let him assist in any of his lines of investigation. And he'd heard nothing from the next room but the door opening and closing, a muted conversation, the door opening and closing again.

What a super sleuth he was. No good in the field. That was why Shar kept him chained to his desk.

Shar . . .

He had the Brandt Institute's number on speed dial. He pressed the button and, when someone answered, asked about his aunt's condition. No change, but she'd had a few visitors and, while tired, had seemed to enjoy them. Was Mr. Ripinsky there? Mick asked. No, he'd left a while ago.

No change. Would there ever be a change?

Had to be!

Mick booted up his laptop and began—obsessively, as he had ever since he'd been told of Shar's diagnosis—to search sites about locked-in syndrome. When that yielded nothing new, he put in a disc of a favorite film—*The X-Files: I Want to Believe*—hoping it would lull him to sleep.

*   *   *

Pop!

The sound brought him awake slowly, as if he were surfacing from the depths of a swimming pool.

Another pop, then silence. A door, the one to his unit's left, swung closed on squeaky hinges. He was off the bed and fully alert within fifteen seconds.

Outside it was still dark and a chill sea wind blew fog inland. At first Mick saw no one, then another door opened and a man stepped out. Craig. His astonished eyes connected with Mick's; he rushed over, grabbed him by the elbow, and shoved him back into his room.

"What the hell're *you* doing here?" Craig demanded.

"Same thing you are. What's happened?"

"I don't know. A popping sound in the next unit—could've been a gunshot."

"I heard it, too."

Craig peered through the partially opened door, his head swiveling from right to left. "Don't think anybody else did. No lights, no people anywhere."

"Then let's check it out."

The door to the unit was unlocked. They pushed through, and Craig nudged the light switch on with his elbow.

Two figures lay sprawled on the bed, naked. They were facing each other, and their heads were destroyed, blood and brain matter splattered on the linens, headboard, and wall. The man held a gun in his limp hand, and the smell of cordite was strong in the small room. No signs of a struggle, just two people . . . shot. Shot dead.

Mick reeled back, gagging, and left the room. Leaned against the railing of the walkway, his head down, breathing heavily. Sweat chilled on his forehead, and he swallowed hard to keep the rising bile down.

God, now he knew why all those nightmares plagued Shar. That scene in the motel room would haunt him till the day he died.

Craig was still inside. After a few seconds he came out, obviously shaken, looked quickly around, and once again dragged Mick into his room. "You okay?" he asked.

"Not really."

"I know, guy, but we've got to move fast. That's Amanda Teller and Paul Janssen in there. Supposed to look like a murder-suicide."

"My God! The supervisor and the state representative?"

"Uh-huh. What I've been working on." Craig's mouth pulled down grimly. "The shit's going to hit the fan in a big way when their bodies're discovered, and we don't want to get splattered with it."

Mick didn't focus on what Craig had said. He asked, "Were they having an affair?"

"No. This was a business meeting. And I think they were murdered and placed like that to make it look like a suicide pact. My damn surveillance tapes must've run out while I was sleeping. The pops we heard indicate the gun was equipped with a silencer, but it's gone now."

"Man, we better call the police."

Craig shook his head. "No, neither of us wants to be here when they're found. And that won't be for a few hours. Since nobody but us heard the shots, it's safe enough to take off, put some distance between this place and us. We'll meet up at Monterey. I know a diner there that's always open."

The thought of food made Mick's stomach lurch and he grimaced.

"Hold on," Craig said. "I know you want to puke, but you'll be surprised how fast your appetite comes back. Besides, you gotta eat. Now, here's what you do: you've paid in advance?"

"Yes."

"Registered under your own name?"

"No."

"Good. Leave the key in the room, roll your bike out of here and up the highway a ways before you start it. The diner in Monterey is called Lulu's, on Munras Avenue. Wait there for me."

"You're not leaving yet?"

"Pretty quick. There're a few things I've got to do."

Mick stood still, numb. Craig gave him a nudge. "Go. Get your stuff and leave now!"

SHARON McCONE

Ma arrived on Hy's arm at ten in the morning. She was wearing a smart blue dress and carrying a bunch of yellow roses—my favorites. But when she looked at me she started to cry and Hy, rolling his eyes, helped her into the chair and took the flowers.

"Can I touch her?" Ma asked him through her tears.

"Of course. She can see you and hear you. You can look into her eyes and ask her yes-or-no questions. One blink yes, two blinks no." He sounded weary, as if he'd repeated this to her many times. "I'm going to get a vase for the roses."

He fled. Ma started to cry. She'd cried all through dinner with Hy last night, he'd told me. The hell of it was, I couldn't put out my arms to hold her, or say something funny that would soon jolly her out of it. The past thirteen days had defined the word "impotence" in depth for me.

Hy came back, removed the dark red roses he'd brought me the day before, and replaced them with Ma's. Their delicate yellow petals reminded me of the ones he'd sent me weekly at the office for years until, as our relationship deepened, he'd changed the standing order to a darker and darker red; they still came—in fact, some might be sitting on my desk at the pier right now.

The pier . . . No, don't think about that now. Bad enough to have these jumbled flashbacks.

Suddenly Ma gave a strangled cry and threw herself on my

chest. Grabbed my head with both hands and stared into my eyes. "You really are there, my precious baby! I know you are!"

I won't be if you crush me!

Hy lifted her off and set her back in the chair. "Kay," he said, "you've got to calm yourself. You're upsetting Sharon."

Sobs. "How can I upset her? She just lies there and . . . Oh!" A wail.

God, I wish I could get up and smack her!

And then, like a messenger of the deity whose name I'd just invoked, my other mother walked into the room. Saskia Blackhawk. She smiled at Hy and me, but went straight to Ma.

"Kay, don't cry. Sharon's here with us. Just ask her if she is."

Ma, her makeup ruined by tears, looked hesitantly at me. "You *are* with us, aren't you, darling?"

I blinked yes.

Ma sank back into the chair, then gave me a tremulous smile.

"Kay," Saskia said, "I noticed a pretty little atrium garden when I came in. Why don't we go out there and talk about what we're going to do for our daughter?"

Ma nodded, clearly eager to be out of my presence. Hy watched them go, shook his head, and said, "Thank God Saskia's plane was on time. I don't think either of us could've taken much more of that . . . caterwauling."

I blinked.

"I have another surprise," he added. "And a pleasant one."

He turned to the door, and a man entered. Slender and stooped, with gray hair in a long ponytail. He held a cowboy hat in his long artist's fingers, and his dark eyes were calm and compassionate as they met mine.

Elwood Farmer, my birth father. The impossible had happened—he'd been lured off the rez in Montana.

JULIA RAFAEL

Sunday morning. Normally she would've taken Tonio to the park and then come home to one of her sister's big dinners. But now she was at the pier, digging deeper into her files, as Shar's intense gaze last night had commanded her to do.

Something always escapes your notice the first few times around. Usually a small thing that helps the big things make sense.

Over and over during her probationary period with the agency, her boss had told her that.

On a legal pad she printed Larry Peeples's name. Linked it with an arrow pointed to Haven Dietz's. Below Larry's she drew another arrow and linked it to Ben Gold, the boyfriend.

Julia paged through the file to the transcript of the initial interview that she'd held here at the pier with Gold. He and Larry had been together two years, and Ben had had dinner with Larry the day before he disappeared. They'd met at work, the Home Showcase in Union Square.

Julia scribbled down, "Reinterview Ben."

Back to Dietz. She'd worked for WKP Associates, a money management firm. She'd been good at her job, monitoring the portfolios of several high-profile clients, and was in line for a promotion at the time of the attack.

The attack had been a particularly vicious one, as indicated by the severity of Dietz's injuries. The police had contacted many of her friends and associates, but none of them could name anyone who held a grudge against her. Julia had reinterviewed those she could reach, but many of them had left the area, and after a year memories had faded.

She picked up the phone and called Dietz to remind her of their appointment to continue their conversation tonight; she'd tried to meet with her last night, but Dietz had refused—it was Saturday and she had plans.

Bullshit, Julia had thought. This from a woman who seldom left her apartment? Dietz was losing interest in the case, and maybe it was a sign that she wanted to put the attack behind her and move on. But if the Dietz investigation had something to do with Shar getting shot, she'd press on in spite of the client's best interests.

Haven sounded surly and hungover when she answered the phone. Probably her plans for the night before had involved a bottle. Yes, all right, Julia could come over that night, but not till after eight. A friend was coming for an early dinner.

Julia agreed, even if it meant another evening without being able to read to Tonio.

She ended the call, then sat back and stared at the thick files.

Not likely that Larry Peeples—with or without the cooperation of Ben Gold—had taken a branch of Home Showcase for 100,000 dollars in small bills. He'd worked in the stockroom, had no access to money. Ben worked the sales desk, but Julia knew from Sophia's experience as a clerk at Safeway that the cash drawer had to balance out to the penny every day. Besides, most people paid by credit card.

She supposed Larry and Ben could've worked a computer scam to skim money, but that took smarts like Mick's or Derek's. Ben— a model and wannabe actor on the side—didn't have that kind of brainpower, and Larry had been described as kind of dim by Haven Dietz. Even Larry's parents seemed aware of his limitations.

So why had he hidden the money in the tack room? And possibly appeared last night to reclaim it?

Maybe he was afraid the bills had been marked, or the serial numbers noted. Maybe he'd left them there till he'd thought it was safe to spend it. Maybe he'd disappeared because he was afraid of being found out. But wasn't six months long enough? Was the quiet, loving son his parents had described the kind of man who could do such a cruel thing to his folks and his lover?

She called Home Showcase and learned that Ben Gold was working the day shift. Then she set out for Union Square.

RAE KELLEHER

Angie Atkins, a prostitute found dead in an alley off Sixth Street three years ago. Angie's friend Callie O'Leary, who had hooked up with a sleazy attorney and abandoned her fleabag hotel room. Rae might never find O'Leary. Sad fact, but women in the sex trade often disappeared or were randomly killed and their bodies never identified. Some simply moved on. Others—the lucky ones—retreated into lives of respectability.

So which kind was Callie?

Rae was sitting at the desk allotted to her in the office shared by Thelia Chen and Diane D'Angelo, Thelia's assistant whom Shar had hired last December. Chen was superefficient, a former analyst at Bank of America, with a wide range of contacts within the city's financial world; she was descended from an old, respected Chinatown family and could tell stories of the history of the Chinese in California in which her own people were personally involved.

D'Angelo, a CPA, was something of a puzzle: she was very reserved, didn't speak of her life outside the office, and generally . . . well, didn't fit with the agency culture. Rae had sneaked a look at her personnel file and found she was a member of a well-to-do Peninsula family, had gone to an exclusive Bay Area private school and to Yale, then worked three years for a major New York City accounting firm. Unspecified personal reasons were cited for her return to the Bay Area. From her address in fashionable Cow

Hollow, Rae assumed she didn't really have to work and was getting a kick out of playing at being a private investigator.

Of course, Rae couldn't criticize her for that: *she* didn't need to work either.

But need wasn't relevant to her situation, or Ricky's. They were both driven people. Poor most of their lives, once they'd found their respective niches they'd poured everything they had into their work. Being able to do the thing you loved was rare—a gift that shouldn't be squandered.

Besides, work had gotten her out of the house on a Sunday when Ricky, two of his band members, four of the kids, and Charlene and her husband, Vic, were having a barbecue.

Talk about extended families. . . .

Angie Atkins, on the other hand, had had no family of any kind, no history. Today's throwaway woman with, probably, only a made-up name that had already faded in the SFPD's files. Impossible to find her killer.

No, not impossible. She was going to close this one. And maybe find a link to Shar's shooting.

MICK SAVAGE

He sat in a booth at Lulu's Diner in Monterey, repeatedly turning his coffee cup in its saucer. In spite of what Craig had told him about one's appetite returning quickly, the smell of bacon, eggs, toast, and pancakes made him queasy. Pictures of the dead man and woman—only flashes, but vivid—kept appearing in his mind.

He'd never venture out into the field again. A desk, a monitor, a keyboard—those were the things he needed to look at. Not bodies and bloodstains. Leave that stuff to the pros with the strong stomachs.

Traffic whizzed by on Munras Avenue, a long street on the edge of the downtown area that seemed mainly populated by motels and eateries. Low-budget tourist heaven. The fog was thick here—although not as thick as farther south—and people were bundled up and walking quickly along the sidewalk. Getaway weekend for a lot of people from the Bay Area, where today the sun was predicted to shine.

This location, Mick reflected, was uncomfortably close to the quaint seaside town of Carmel, where he and Sweet Charlotte had gone for a supposedly romantic winter vacation. They'd checked into a little bed-and-breakfast on a side street, had lunch at an expensive trattoria, window-shopped. He'd bought her a necklace she'd admired at a jewelry store—all the time thinking of how surprised she'd be at the diamond ring in his jacket pocket—and at sunset, on the white sand beach at the end of Ocean Avenue where wind-warped cypress grew, he'd proposed to her.

She'd said no. In fact she'd been planning to wait till the end of the weekend to tell him she'd be moving out of his condo next week. She needed some space, she said.

Mick never took the ring out of his pocket. They'd walked silently back to the B&B, collected their things, and driven straight back to the city. Next day, Charlotte had started packing her belongings; she'd already found a place on Potrero Hill. Mick returned the ring to Tiffany's later that week.

And had vowed never again to set foot in Carmel.

Now he tried to blank out, lose himself in the flow of vehicles on Munras, but unpleasant images of both the crime scene and the abortive trip to Carmel persisted. He was grateful when he saw Craig's SUV pull into the lot.

Craig came inside, looking like the ordinary tourist in search of breakfast. He raised a hand to Mick and came back to the booth. A waitress appeared quickly, and he ordered something called the Seaside Special, raised his eyebrows at Mick.

"Toast," Mick said. "No, make that an English muffin. And a glass of milk." When the server departed, he leaned toward Craig and asked, "Took you a long time."

"Flat tire a few miles down the coast."

Mick glanced around; nobody was paying any attention to their conversation. "What were those things you had to do in Big Sur?"

"Take another look at . . . the people. And search for a document she made him sign."

"That . . . thing, you're sure it wasn't murder-suicide?"

"I'd stake my life on it. When I went back to the room I took a closer look at them. Needle marks on their necks, probably some kind of fast-acting sedative. Made it easier to move him to her room and set up the scene beforehand. Any good ME will spot them immediately."

"So the shooter doesn't care if it comes out that it was murder?"

"All he wanted was that document—he got it—and a clean getaway. The initial news reports will create a commotion that'll overshadow what the autopsy reveals. And by that time the story'll be off page one."

Their food arrived. Mick took a sip of milk. Better.

He asked, "But how did the shooter get in? They wouldn't've left their doors unlocked."

"No dead bolts—remember? Those old snap locks are flimsy. Or he could've gotten hold of a passkey; that clerk who checked me in didn't look as if she was above taking a bribe."

"You think it was a man who did it?"

"A man, or maybe a woman with a male partner. Janssen was big, would've been hard for most women to carry. Hard to drag, even."

Mick bit into his English muffin. If it stayed down, he might consider ordering a real breakfast. "So why're you investigating Teller and Janssen?" he asked.

"I'll tell you that when we get to a more secure location."

SHARON McCONE

E lwood sat in the chair next to me, his gaze gentle on mine.
"I can feel your spirit, Daughter," he said. "I can feel your
fear. But also your determination and hope."

*Well, that's a hell of a lot better than wailing and hurling yourself
on my chest and nearly crushing me.*

"I can also feel your anger. At the one who did this to you,
but—worse—at those like Kay who indulge their own emotions
at the expense of yours. Or those who treat you as a person forever
changed."

I blinked once.

"You must let go of that anger. People are fallible, often weak, but
they love you. Focus it instead on the one who did this to you."

Blink.

Elwood touched my arm. First time I'd ever had comforting
physical contact with my birth father. Tears blurred my gaze.

"Anger is powerful and good, if not misused," he added. "You
must tap into your roots, feel the rage and the power of those who
have lived before you."

I blinked, and the tears trickled down my face.

"Your great-grandmother, I understand, knew anger and
became a warrior woman. She found the courage to leave the
Indian agent who had taken her for his own and abused her,
to accompany a kind white man to California and build a new
life. Your grandmother on my side was a woman who accepted

nothing—poverty, lack of education, abandonment—on other than her own terms. Your mother, Saskia, she's brave and smart, has argued before the United States Supreme Court—and won every case. And your people, the Shoshone, go on and on against all odds."

My emotions were on a roller-coaster ride again. Elwood's hand touched my forehead, then brushed my tears away.

"It's in your blood, Daughter," he said. "You will continue to fight this, and you will win."

I must have slept because I didn't remember Elwood leaving. One minute he was talking to me, the next I felt someone holding a cool cloth to my face and opened my eyes to see Saskia. As ever I was struck by our resemblance to each other and to my half sister Robin. Put the three of us together in a photo, and you'd see one individual aging well through different stages of life.

She smiled at me. "Rough morning?"

I blinked.

"Your mother is . . . not emotionally stable these days, and your condition has somewhat unhinged her. Your doctor prescribed a mild tranquilizer, and Hy took her back to her hotel. She'll be here again tomorrrow."

Why is she unstable?

Saskia had seen the question in my eyes. "Her husband has been diagnosed with bladder cancer. And she has been having dizzy spells and weakness in her limbs. Most of her problems, I think, are in response to his condition."

Ma hasn't told me any of this! Nobody's told me. What's wrong with them? Do they think I can't take upsetting news?

Again Saskia understood. "Neither of them wanted anyone to know or to worry. Just as you wish you could go through this ordeal in private. But that's a mistake, Sharon. Your life and health don't belong exclusively to you; those who love you have a big stake in your future."

Obligations to others? Fuck that!

"And they can help you through this."

Well . . . maybe.

Saskia and Elwood, they were both so insightful in their different ways. And Pa was wise, too: he had left me the documentation to find out who I really was. Ma: she took me in as a tiny baby, loved me, and never treated me as if I weren't her flesh and blood.

Hy—he was and always would be my lover and my best friend.

My stepfather, Melvin Hunt. Bladder cancer—my God! He and Ma would need my support, but how could I give it to them from a hospital bed? I *had* to get better.

Rae and Ricky and the kids. Especially Mick. Ted and Neal. Craig and Adah. Julia. Charlene, Vic, Patsy, and John. Patrick. All the others who were family, bloodlines not withstanding.

Saskia is right: my life belongs to them as much as it does to me.

My eyelids were getting heavy again. My birth mother said, "Rest now. You're not alone, Sharon. Not ever."

JULIA RAFAEL

Union Square was teeming with people clutching bags from the department stores and specialty shops. Many were tourists who had come unprepared for a San Francisco summer and shivered in shorts and T-shirts. In spite of their discomfort, the scene was lively. Cable cars rumbled and clanged on Powell Street, people hanging off the sides and, in some cases, waving energetically. Pigeons flocked to a woman who stood in the square, tossing them bread. There were long lines at the discount ticket office for plays and concerts. Julia could feel the crackling energy.

Although she'd lived most of her life in the city, as a child and young adult Julia had seldom come downtown; the Mission district was her turf—a closely defined and confined neighborhood. Many of San Francisco's poorer areas were like small cities unto themselves, their residents rarely venturing past their limits, except to go to work—if they had work.

Besides, what would've been the point in coming here? Bus fare was expensive, and Mission district families like Julia's didn't have the money to shop in the stores, to eat in the restaurants, to go to the theaters. She remembered one time when her sister Sophia had brought her to see the annual Christmas tree all decorated in the square: the tree had been nice, but it was the people who fascinated her—well dressed and carefree, the women smelling of expensive perfumes and the men of aftershave, many of them getting out of cabs and limousines or turning their beautiful cars over to valet parkers. It was an exciting experience, but after enjoying a gingerbread man Sophia bought her from a street vendor, Julia had been glad to go home to the Mission. It was where she felt comfortable.

But now, she realized, all that had changed. Sure, she had a crappy car, but she also had parked it in the garage under the square, on her expense account. She was wearing a good leather jacket—almost paid for—and a pair of stylish jeans and boots. Best of all, she was a woman with a business to go about, and a State of California private investigator's license to prove it. And last night—much as she'd hated the silence—she'd spent the night as a guest of a Sonoma Valley vintner.

Don't let it go to your head, chica, *you're only the hired help.*

But it was a lot better than what she used to do when men hired her.

The light changed, and she crossed the intersection. The big Home Showcase store on Stockton Street was crowded with shoppers inspecting the specialty food items, glassware, china, and linens. Julia angled toward the sales desk, briefly slowing her pace to admire a set of candlesticks that she knew Sophia would love. Maybe she'd buy them for her birthday; that way they could use them on the Thanksgiving table. . . .

Ben Gold was behind the desk, wrapping up a cut-glass vase and a bunch of multicolored dried flowers. He handed the shopping bag to the customer and turned expectantly to Julia. His smile faded when he saw her, and his handsome features sharpened; alarm showed in his bright blue eyes.

"Is it news?" he asked. "About Larry?"

"Can you take a break?"

He glanced around, motioned to one of the other employees on the floor. "Fifteen minutes. No more."

They went out onto the sidewalk and stood beside a window displaying slow cookers and books on using them. Ben crossed his arms on his chest, an intricately braided silver bracelet on his left wrist gleaming in the sun. He tilted his blond head and waited as if for some crushing blow.

Julia said, "I haven't found Larry, no. But something's come up and I need to ask you some additional questions."

"What happened to your nose? And your eyes—they're kinda black."

"Car accident." She waved dismissively.

"You oughta drive more carefully. Bad karma around your agency. Your boss—I read in the paper that she was shot. How is she?"

"She's . . . not good."

"Is she going to live?"

"They don't know. Right now she's stabilized."

He shook his head. "This city, the violence. Does she remember what happened to her?"

"I don't know. She can't communicate at present. About my questions . . . ?"

"Yes?"

"Was Larry happy in his work here?"

"Not really. I mean, stocking shelves—how many of us are content with that kind of work? At least I get to interact with customers and I've got outside interests and future prospects. I think I told you I'm moving to LA next week. It's only a couple of commercials, but I've got an agent and he promises me more work. But Larry, he'd been kicked out of three colleges and had no future except going back to the Sonoma Valley and learning the winemaking business under his father's thumb."

"Are those your words or his—'under his father's thumb'?"

"His."

"I thought he was close to his parents."

"He was, but the life up there can be confining, and his dad can be extremely demanding."

"But still he'd given his notice here and was moving home."

"It was the money, that's what finally got to him."

"The money?"

"Well, sure. That's a successful vineyard his old man has, and very valuable land. Besides, his parents offered him a bribe to come home—a hundred thousand dollars, cash. Larry claimed he was going to collect and then the two of us would head for Tahiti or South America, but I didn't believe him."

"You didn't tell me this before."

Gold averted his eyes, fiddling with his bracelet, a flush spreading up his neck. "It's tough to admit you've been dumped. But dump me was what Larry did. Took his hundred thou and split without me. He's probably having a great life someplace—with somebody else."

Except that the hundred thousand had been hidden in his parents' tack room since he disappeared.

And Julia seriously doubted it had come from the Peeples.

RAE KELLEHER

The lead she'd been seeking was in Angie Atkins's file, buried deep, where Rae's eyes—tired since the night Shar was shot—hadn't noticed it before. A notation in the police report of the personal property on Atkins's body: "1 high-school class ring."

Jesus, why hadn't the cops followed up on that? And what high school was it from?

Sunday. She had only two contacts on the SFPD, and she doubted either would be on duty or eager to access the information. But Adah could: she was no longer on the job, but she could navigate the system.

"Hell yes," Adah said when Rae called her. "Anything to narrow down who attacked Shar. But it's totally illegal. Will you visit me in prison?"

"Every week, with a file baked into hash brownies."

"Good woman."

Rae hung up the receiver and drummed her fingertips on the desktop while looking around the office. Water stains at the top of the far wall, carpet showing wear. Today when she'd come up the stairs to the catwalk they'd creaked ominously. Shar, with the help of her powerful attorney friend Glenn Solomon—who seemed to have something on everybody in city government—had negotiated a good deal with the port commission for an extended lease, but maybe it was time to think of moving on. She'd have to talk to Shar about it—

Shit! She couldn't.

Phone. Adah.

"The ring was from Acalanes High School, class of oh-six."

"Acalanes?"

"East Bay. Near Walnut Creek, I think."

"How'd they miss that?"

"Dead hooker, overload of cases, and they probably didn't care all that much."

"*You* wouldn't've missed it."

"I don't know, maybe toward the end I would've. I was getting to the point where I didn't give a shit, either."

"Well, thanks for running the check."

"No problem. Craig's been off on some lead since Friday night. I got so bored this afternoon that I went to the animal shelter and came back with two kittens."

"I was wondering if you'd ever get another after Charley died. And now two!"

"Tortoiseshells—sisters, around six months old. Lots of energy. They're tearing the place apart."

"What're you calling them?"

"That One and the Other One, till Craig gets back to consult."

"Well, good luck. And thanks again."

Damn! Why had she stumbled on this lead on a Sunday? In summer, no less, when school was out and staff members only came in to work on a sporadic basis?

Rae broke the connection and turned to her keyboard. Googled Acalanes High School, and got its address on Pleasant Hill Road in the East Bay suburb of Lafayette. The school's site had a list of people to contact for various types of information: Rae copied the page. Then she began to search the East Bay phone books.

"Information on students and former students is confidential," Jane Koziol, counseling secretary of the high school, said when

Rae reached her at her home number in Walnut Creek. "But if this girl has been murdered . . . You say you want me to identify a photograph?"

"Yes. Apparently she wasn't using her real name. Her family hasn't been notified of her death, and the closure would be very important to them."

". . . And you're a licensed private investigator?"

"Working with the Bay Area Victims' Advocates."

"All right. I have a fax machine. Send me your credentials and the photograph. If the girl graduated in oh-six, it's likely I'll recognize her."

"I can fax a copy of my license and the photo in a few minutes."

"Fine. Where can I reach you?"

Rae gave the agency's phone number.

"I'll be in touch."

When Koziol called back an hour later, she sounded shaken. "I'm sorry it took so long to get back to you, but I decided to talk with my attorney first."

"No problem. It's what I would've done."

"The girl in the photograph is Alicia Summers. I . . . God, I can't believe it!"

"What can you tell me about her?"

"She disappeared a couple of months after she graduated. The family is well-to-do, they live in the Lafayette hills, and her father's a lawyer, involved in the Pro Terra Party. You've heard of them?"

"Environmentalists? Aren't they the ones who run candidates on a third-party basis?"

"Yes. Alicia was a good student until her senior year, then her grades fell off radically. I tried to work with her, but she wasn't responsive. All she would tell me was that school didn't matter any more, nothing did."

"Did you ask her why?"

"Of course I did. But she refused to talk about it."

"What about her parents—did you consult with them?"

"Her mother. She complained of Alicia's unexplained absences on weekends and sometimes on weeknights."

"Had she asked her daughter about those?"

"Yes—and she'd gotten the same response I did. After a while she didn't press the issue. If anything, she seemed . . . intimidated by Alicia."

"Intimidated? In what way?"

Koziol hesitated. "Alicia had the upper hand in the relationship. I think her mother felt that if she confronted her, she'd lose her."

"And the father? Did you speak with him?"

"No. Lee Summers is too important a man to speak with a mere high-school counselor."

"Did you consider sexual abuse as a factor in Alicia's problems?"

"Oddly enough, I didn't. I know it's the first thing a counselor would suspect, but from her body language and the way she talked, it didn't fit into the equation."

"What did?"

". . . Disillusionment. Something in her experience had opened her eyes to the world in a way a person of her age and development couldn't deal with except by giving up."

"I didn't tell you before, but she was working as a prostitute in the city when she died."

"Well, I can't say I'm surprised. That's giving up as much as any woman can, isn't it?"

SHARON McCONE

*T*his evening I'm working on moving my toes. Toes, because dexterity on the rudders with one's feet is essential to flying.

First one, then another. Concentrating hard, because I'm going to beat this paralysis. What Elwood said about my great-grandmother, how she became a warrior woman—I'll never forget that.

I'm at war, too.

I closed my eyes, pictured my right toe. Willed it to move. Nothing.

Okay, I thought, *left toe.*

Still nothing.

Frustration welled up again. Why was I putting myself through this? It was hopeless. I was trapped inside myself, a well-wrapped mummy, with no sensation except my raging emotions. And those . . .

Once, in a rented beachfront place on the island of Hawaii, Hy and I had been awakened by an earthquake. The house had shaken violently, gone still, then shaken again almost as hard. We looked outside, saw the sea was placid, but could feel its roiling potential. Fled to higher ground, along with all the neighbors.

The tsunami we'd feared never happened, although we later found out that we were within three miles of the quake's epicenter at sea. But its innate rage and desire to destroy everything in its path charged the air, and a day later we cut our stay short and returned home.

Now a rage like that had invaded my body and threatened to consume what remained of my rationality.

What had happened to me? Where was the woman who had soared above the Sierras and Crater Lake, thrilled to controlled spins, loved and married a man whom some people, myself included, considered "still dangerous"? The woman who had braved a paramilitary encampment, a clandestine border crossing, a child rescue on an isolated Caribbean island?

Where was *I*?

No. Don't you go there.

Right toe. Concentrate.

. . . *Can't.*

Wait a while and try again. For now, concentrate on the verbal reports given to you today.

Julia had said that Larry Peeples told his lover his parents were giving him a hundred thousand dollars to return home and learn the winery business; instead he was planning to run off with Ben Gold and the money. But that hadn't happened.

Rae had identified the hooker who'd been stabbed in the alley off Sixth Street. She was the daughter of a well-to-do and politically connected East Bay family. Rae had notified the SFPD who, after verifying her information, would contact the parents. Rae hoped to meet with them tomorrow, but till then was pursuing leads about the father's involvement in the Pro Terra Party.

The Pro Terra Party. Hy didn't like them. They ran candidates for local office around the state on an environmental stance, but he was dubious as to their motives and actual commitment to the movement. A stealthy money and power grab cloaked in altruism, he suspected. They lost more often than they won, but they were making gains: their most notable success had been with the election of State Representative Paul Janssen of San Francisco.

It would be interesting to see what Rae reported tomorrow.

Nothing from Mick or Craig. Curious.

I was tired. Too many visitors in too little time. Too many things to absorb. Soon Hy would arrive for his evening visit. I'd rest till then.

No, I wouldn't. Not until I tried again . . . and again . . . and again to make my toes move.

HY RIPINSKY

He was going to be late seeing Shar, but she would understand. The one thing that had remained constant through all of this was their mutual psychic connection. It had been strong from almost the first day they'd met, and while it may have faltered at times during their relationship, it now tugged at him, taut as wire. He knew it tugged at her, too.

All afternoon he'd been at home, on the phone and Internet, talking and e-mailing with friends and informants around the world. He'd run searches trying to connect any of the cases the agency folks were working with his wife's shooting. No definite links, but a whisper here and there.

Yes, I've heard the theory that she was attacked by someone look-ing for information . . . No, it probably wasn't personal, but who knows? . . . Sometimes people are in the wrong place at the wrong time . . . She did have enemies. Couldn't've helped but have, in her position . . . She's received a lot of high-profile publicity over the years . . . That pier was featured in a nationally syndicated piece about unusual working environments . . . Maybe somebody was fol-lowing her. That classic MG she insists on driving is distinctive . . . Let me call around to some of my contacts and get back to you . . .

Hy got into his vintage blue Mustang, which was parked in the driveway, backed out, and flicked on the radio as he turned down the street.

News broadcast. Special report.

San Francisco Board of Supes President Amanda Teller and State Representative Paul Janssen had been found dead in an apparent murder-suicide at a lodge near Big Sur. Mystery surrounded the crimes: as yet there was no explanation as to what they were doing there. Although they had checked into separate units, they were found together on Teller's bed. Stay tuned for further details. . . .

Amanda Teller.

Hadn't Shar done some work for her about a year ago?

Worth checking out. And right away.

Shar would have to wait for him a little longer.

He called Ted Smalley at home and then set his course for Pier 24½, where Ted could access the records from the office computer system.

SHARON McCONE

I was expecting Hy but it was Mick and Craig who came into my room. They were arguing in the soft voices that this place seemed to bring out in people. Well, most people. Not Ma and not me; she shrieked and I had no voice.

Mick said, "*This* is the secure location where we're gonna talk?"

"As secure as they get, man."

"But what about Shar? She's sick, she needs her rest."

Stop talking about me as if I weren't here!

"She also needs to hear this, and I don't want to go over it twice." Craig came around the bed, looked me in the eyes. "Shar? You okay to listen to a long story?"

I blinked. Damn right I was. Maybe my body wasn't spearheading the investigation this time, but my mind was as sharp as ever.

Both of them sat down, Craig in the armchair and Mick in a folding chair he dragged in from outside.

Craig said, "Amanda Teller, president of the Board of Supes, and State Representative Paul Janssen were shot to death in a motel near Big Sur early this morning."

I wanted to exclaim, "What? Why?" All I could do was rivet my gaze on his and wait.

"It was set up to look like a murder-suicide, but I don't think it was. More likely a double homicide."

He went on to tell me what he and Mick had witnessed at the

Spindrift Lodge, ending with, "You know I've been investigating possible malfesance at city hall for the mayor's office. I think these killings are connected to that."

I remembered the case. One of the mayor's closest aides and confidants, Jim Yatz, had summoned me to his office in early June and asked me to take on an undercover operation. He didn't specifically know what the mayor was looking for, but there was some concern about certain confidential documents going missing. Yatz provided me with a list of them; they seemed innocuous enough to me: drafts of general plans for city land use, an updated rent control proposition, budget proposals. Some of the documents had been handwritten in draft, others were computer files that had subsequently been deleted. I offered the services of our computer forensics department to recover them, but Yatz turned that down. Find out who was doing it, that was all the mayor wanted.

Yatz, a burly, dark-haired man in a well-tailored blue suit, had struck me as poorly informed about the missing documents and the mayor's concerns. And he was a gatekeeper—no way I was going to get in to see the mayor personally, even though I'd met him a number of times at environmental fund-raisers Hy and I had attended. Finally, though, I decided we'd take the case, if for no other reason than to protect the city's administration, which, for the most part, I supported.

Since I was too well known around the Bay Area, I suggested to Yatz that Craig handle the investigation. But after he and I met with Yatz, we decided Craig had too many contacts in city government to go unrecognized either; he would supervise and send in someone else to do the actual fieldwork. Diane D'Angelo, our newest hire, was his choice because of her polish and business background.

For two weeks Diane worked in the mayor's office as a temporary replacement for his executive secretary, who was on vacation. She saw nothing out of the ordinary, and no documents disappeared until her last day there. This one was classified as a confidential communication between Amanda Teller and the mayor; no details of its contents were given to us. I ended my direct involvement at that point, though I'd kept myself apprised by reading Craig's reports, which basically posited that someone was playing political games of no consequence.

Well, games or not, this one had had monumental consequences. Amanda Teller, a forty-year-old woman with an impressive record of service to the community, and Paul Janssen, age fifty-two, a maverick who was challenging the status quo in our mired-down state government, were both dead. And under circumstances that could destroy their legacies.

Craig went on, "Do you recognize the name Harvey Davis?"

Amanda Teller's campaign manager and a close aide. I blinked.

"Three weeks ago he contacted me. He'd heard I was working for the mayor and said that he had information that would shake up local government. He didn't want money for it and he didn't want to be named as the one who blew the whistle. He passed along minor details about Teller—with whom he seemed very disillusioned. Frankly, I thought he was getting off on acting like he had important inside information. Then on Friday he told me Teller and Janssen were scheduled to meet at Big Sur yesterday. Now they're both dead, Davis, too."

Craig continued his narrative, telling me about the Davis hit and his subsequent visit to the man's condo. When he detailed the explicit sexual content of the DVDs he'd found there my senses reeled and I went into a kind of brain lock.

Craig said, "I don't know where he got those DVDs, but I suspect Teller had copies, too. The conversation between her and Janssen that I recorded reeks of blackmail."

I just stared at him.

Mick said, "She's exhausted. Let's come back in the morning."

I'm not exhausted, just shocked. Because of that investigation I did for Amanda Teller a year ago, I may have set this thing in motion. And I've got no way of communicating what I know.

"... Right," Craig said. He stood. "Tonight Mick and I will go over the DVDs and my surveillance tapes. We'll be back tomorrow with a more detailed report. We'll also play the videos for you."

I blinked, then closed my eyes. I needed time to process this.

Feet clanging on metal—my feet going up the catwalk at the pier. Echoes resonating off the flat roof.

Elusive, flickering light. Sudden motion.

Collision with a strong body. Falling, reaching out.

Fingertips grazing metal.

Flash!

Chains?

Pain. Darkness.

Now. A life without speech or motion.

The silent scream welled up, and I cursed what I'd become.

JULIA RAFAEL

Flashing lights disturbed the dusk as she drove along Twentieth Avenue in the city's normally peaceful Richmond district, going to her appointment with Haven Dietz. She felt a prickling at the base of her spine as she realized the emergency vehicles were congregated at Dietz's three-story brick apartment house.

People milled around outside the police barriers. Julia pulled her car into a red zone near a fire hydrant and ran down the sidewalk, pushed past gawkers, then stopped when she saw a gurney with a body bag being loaded into an ambulance. A young, heavyset cop was standing guard behind the yellow crime scene tape. She went up to him, and . . . oh, shit.

Matthew Griffin. He used to work out of the Mission district precinct, and he'd busted her two times for prostitution.

He recognized her at once. "Julia Rafael. What're you doing here?"

She took out one of her agency business cards and extended it to him. "Working. A woman who lives in that building is my client."

Surprisingly, he took a long look at the card. "I heard you went straight. That's a good agency. McCone has always been somebody who takes a chance on people. How's she doing since the shooting?"

"About the same. She's aware, but can't move or speak."

"Jesus, what a shame."

He didn't know the half of it. Shar had given her the chance of a lifetime, had stood by her when she almost blew it. She owed her—and then some.

Julia let out a deep breath, asked, "Who's the victim?"

"Woman named Haven Dietz."

"Oh, no . . ."

"She your client?"

"Yes."

He raised the tape. "That man over there in the black coat is Lt. Dave Morrison. Tell him what you know about this."

She ducked under the tape, moved forward. Griffin said, "Julia?"

"Yes?"

"I'm glad you turned your life around."

"Thank you. I am, too."

Lt. Morrison knew nothing of her history and treated her as a professional. He glanced curiously at her scabbed-over nose and blackened eyes, but instead of commenting he listened to her account of the Haven Dietz case and then took her up to the apartment. It had been searched, Dietz's belongings dumped from drawers and hurled around, and there were bloodstains on the carpet and a spatter pattern on the wall. Shot by an intruder, the lieutenant said.

Looking at the bloody wall made Julia gag, and Morrison gave her a concerned look.

Well, Shar would have gagged, too, maybe, but she wouldn't've thrown up, and Julia wasn't going to either.

She swallowed hard, asked, "Did she surprise a burglar?"

"On the surface it would appear that way. But experience tells me someone was looking for something specific."

The hundred thou hidden in the Peepleses' tack room?

She said, "I had an appointment with Dietz for eight o'clock." She checked her watch. "Right about now. I wanted to make it earlier, but she said she was having someone over for dinner. Any sign of that?"

"Nothing's been cooked, and there're no takeout containers.

I'd say that kitchen hasn't been used for anything other than microwaving and coffee-making in quite a while. We'll check it out more thoroughly. You have any idea what the perp might've been looking for?"

Julia shook her head.

"Another theory I have is that her attacker returned to finish his job."

"After a year?"

Morrison shrugged. "It was a vicious attack, indicating extreme anger or psychosis. In the minds of people like that . . . Well, for a lot of them, it's never finished until the victim's dead."

"He used a knife last time. Would he have been likely to switch to a gun?"

"You can't predict what people like that'll do."

Julia looked around the trashed apartment, blocking out the bloodstains. The furnishings were old and worn; there were no pictures or mementoes; it felt like the lair of an animal who had dug in and was waiting to die.

And now she had.

RAE KELLEHER

The Pro Terra Party. Founded in 2002 by environmentalists Cheryl Fitzgerald and Don Beckman. They'd had a falling-out in 2004, and Beckman quit the party; Fitzgerald left in 2006, for unspecified personal reasons. Since then Pro Terra had been run by a board of directors, of which Lee Summers, the dead woman's father, was chairman. Their most notable political win had been Paul Janssen's election to the state house of representatives in 2008.

Rae Googled Cheryl Fitzgerald. The woman had been flying below the search engine's radar since she left the party and took an executive position with a Silicon Valley firm that developed alternative energy sources. Don Beckman had died of a heart attack in 2005. Rae went to one of the search engines the agency subscribed to for more information on Fitzgerald. She was still with Alternative Resources, whose office address was in Cupertino. Rae noted that down, then did a search for Lee Summers.

He had an impressive background: bachelor's degree in prelaw from Stanford, law degree from Harvard. He'd made partner at one of San Francisco's prestigious appeals firms in record time. His personal life was unblemished: he'd been married to his wife, Senta, for twenty-four years; was a regular churchgoer; was a member of two country clubs; served on the boards of various charities. Alicia had been the couple's only child. Five years ago Summers had cut back on his legal practice to devote his energy to the Pro Terra Party, and had been instrumental in Representative Paul Janssen's victory.

All squeaky-clean. Which made Rae uncomfortable. Everybody had something to hide. She certainly did.

Well, maybe that was specious reasoning. If she Googled herself, there would be no mention that in her teens she had been the primo slut of her hometown, Santa Maria. But the details of her very public affair with Ricky would be duly noted. . . .

She moved on to another search engine and dug deeper.

Aha! In 2008 Lee Summers's wife had filed for divorce, but withdrawn the petition two weeks later. Irreconcilable differences had apparently been reconciled. Or a compromise—given that he was involved in an intense political campaign—had been made. Just about the time Alicia had left home and become a prostitute here in the city.

Maybe that high-school counselor's intuitions were wrong. Maybe Rae should rethink the abuse angle.

The phone rang. Rae grabbed it before the call could go to the office machine. Jane Koziol, the Acalanes High School counselor she'd just been thinking of.

"I've been in touch with Alicia's mother, Senta Summers," she said. "She'd like to talk with you. Would tomorrow afternoon at two be okay?"

"Of course." Abuse, just as she'd suspected.

Koziol gave her directions to the Summerses' house in the Lafayette hills and said she'd meet her there.

The timing was perfect. In the morning Rae could drive to Cupertino and appear at Cheryl Fitzgerald's office first thing, when the woman's and her gatekeepers' guards were apt to be low, and go from there to Lafayette for the meeting with Mrs. Summers.

HY RIPINSKY

T he file on the Teller investigation is gone," Ted said to Hy.
"Shit."

"I happen to know a very capable computer forensics expert who can retrieve it."

"Mick? He's been incommunicado since last night."

"Derek's almost as good as he is." Ted was already on the phone, hitting the fast dial. "Hey, Derek, I need you at the pier . . . Forensic job on our own system . . . Okay, see you then." He replaced the receiver and said to Hy, "He'll be here in half an hour."

Hy was silent, distracted.

"You okay?"

"Do I look okay?"

"No."

"Neither do you." Ted's Western-style shirt was rumpled, and he hadn't trimmed his usually neat goatee.

Ted said, "None of us is. Shar . . . it scares me to death. Neal and I went by today, but they wouldn't let us see her—doctors, nurses, visitors backed up out the door."

"Try late at night or early in the morning. There're no restrictions on visiting hours."

"But I don't want to disturb her."

"Believe me, you won't. In spite of not being able to move or talk, her energy's still high. Seeing the people she loves keeps her going."

Ted nodded. Hy knew he wanted to ask about Shar's condition, but was hesitating because he thought it would upset him.

He said, "As recently as a few days ago I wouldn't have believed it, but McCone's not only fully aware, she's working her own case."

"What? How?"

"She's taking verbal reports from everybody, and I can tell she's focused on the facts and theories they're giving her. I wouldn't be surprised if she's the one who puts it all together and IDs the perp. And then finds a way to communicate it to the rest of us."

"My God. You can't stop the woman, can you?"

"I don't know. I've never dared try."

"Okay," Derek Ford said, "I've got it."

The tall, slender Eurasian leaned forward, gazing intently at the computer screen, his thick black hair flopping onto his forehead. He hit the save command, said, "All yours," and stood. He was urban chic, perfectly groomed and outfitted, even on Sunday, with a tattoo of linked scorpions around his neck and numerous silver earrings.

Hy took the chair Derek had vacated. On the screen was the first page of the standard agency report form: client name, address, phone numbers; case number; operative assigned. Client request: deep background on Lee Summers, the Pro Terra Party, and Representative Paul Janssen. The client: the late Amanda Teller.

Hy scrolled down and read on.

SHARON McCONE

Julia and Rae arrived with their reports shortly after Craig and Mick left.

My night nurse, Melissa, preceded them, asking if I was up to having more visitors. I blinked. The frequency of visitors tired me, but it also made me feel a connection to the world I'd involuntarily left behind.

They were still there at ten o'clock when Hy arrived with the information that the file on the background investigations Amanda Teller had requested last year had been deleted from the office's system but recovered by Derek. Hy had read it and found it was a simple background check on people Teller had considered potential political allies or adversaries.

But it had been deleted. Now I had a lot more to process.

If I could talk, or even write, I would've brainstormed with the three of them. Explained the connections I sensed, even if I couldn't back them up. Asked them to look for the missing pieces. But for some reason Julia wasn't reading the signals I was trying to give her with my eyes—probably exhausted from nonstop working. And Rae was reading too much into them. It made me afraid for her; she had a tendency to stray unprepared into dangerous territory.

Hy, on the other hand, understood. We were closely attuned to each other, as always. "You're putting something together, but you need more facts."

Blink.

"Well, maybe tomorrow . . ." He lapsed into silence as Rae and Julia gathered their things and left.

Hy looked discouraged, slouched in the armchair, his hair tousled and his cheeks stubbled. His cellular rang, and he checked it, said he had to take the call, and went out into the corridor. Since the shooting my hearing had become more acute—a compensation for the loss of other functions. Hy probably thought he was out of my earshot.

"Weathers, what d'you want? . . . No, nothing yet . . . I said I'd call you if I had a problem. Where did you get this number? . . . Well, don't call it again."

Weathers.

There was a pilot at North Field by that name. Flew a small jet, and Hy had always gone out of his way to avoid him. Come to think of it, Weathers went out of his way to avoid Hy. So why was Weathers calling him now?

I tried to remember what Hy had told me about the man. Couldn't come up with anything. If he had talked about Weathers it'd been a long time ago and I hadn't retained any of it.

Hy returned, sat back down. Instead of explaining the phone call, he said, "I'm going to sleep here tonight. Your brother's driving me crazy. He keeps concocting preposterous revenge schemes for when we find out who did this to you."

Revenge . . .

And right then I remembered that I did know something about Weathers—first name Len. Hy had known him in Thailand, was surprised when he turned up in the Bay Area. Avoided him because he suspected Weathers had become a professional killer.

Oh God, no, Hy! Don't do it that way!

MONDAY, JULY 21

HY RIPINSKY

He'd seen the bewilderment in Shar's eyes when he reentered her room; probably she'd overheard his conversation and was trying to figure out who Len Weathers was. Alarm had soon replaced bewilderment. She'd tried with her eyes to get him to talk about his involvement with the man, but he'd avoided her unvoiced questions, pretending to doze. He had stayed in the chair beside her bed until she slept with decreasing restlessness. When he slipped out at first light she seemed less fitful.

The institute was close to Land's End, a favorite spot of theirs because it resembled the wild, rocky coast at Touchstone. The westernmost promontory was called Point Lobos, after the sea lions—once called sea wolves—who now made their resting place at Seal Rock, offshore from the historic Cliff House restaurant. The shadowy cypress, pungent-smelling eucalyptus, and miles of coastal views made for a stunningly beautiful and peaceful setting—especially this early in the morning.

Hy drove there and took the trail down the bluff to the large viewing platform above the point. The sun was cresting the city's hills, suffusing the sky with an orange-pink color. The open sea spread before him, the Farallon Islands faintly visible through the mist in the distance. A foghorn bellowed its melancholy message. Hy sat on a bench by the railing and did some soul-searching.

His past had been violent, that was true. The post-Vietnam

era in Southeast Asia bred despicable activity, especially when you were in a kill-or-be-killed situation. He flashed on the memory of the bodies of the Laotian family attempting to escape to the US, frozen in the skin of the plane because they hadn't listened to his instructions about not removing their heavy outerwear while concealed there. That hadn't been his fault, but the massacre in the jungle, where he'd been forced against his will to turn his gun on his own passengers . . . Maybe if he'd been smarter, more receptive to the signals he was getting that day—

Old recriminations. No use dwelling on them.

In the years since then he'd married a good woman, Julie Spaulding, who was devoted to environmental causes. He'd become devoted, too, still sat on the board of the foundation she'd funded in her will. But when Julie died of multiple sclerosis, as they'd both known would eventually happen, he'd turned to radical environmentalism, taking out his anger at her loss in violent protests and demonstrations. Spent more time in jail than your average boy from the high desert country.

That had changed when he met Shar. Well, not totally: he'd been arrested the next March in Siskiyou County for disorderly conduct during an anti-logging demonstration. Fortunately, the charges were dropped.

But still he'd changed. . . . Her love had changed him. He'd been sure of it. He was sure of it still.

So what had he been thinking, contacting a killer like Weathers?

Not thinking: indulging in blind rage. Find the shooter, send Weathers to deliver him, then take his time killing him. Make it slow and painful. Make sure the bastard knew exactly what he had coming to him—and why.

And what would that make *him*?

Hy stared into the mist receding over the sea, trying to avoid the question. But he couldn't do it. The answers were too clear-cut.

Killing the shooter would make him no better than Weathers.

It would mean that he was unchanged after all, the same man he'd always been, the side of him he'd always hated.

No. He wasn't like Weathers, couldn't let himself act as Weathers did.

If he did, it would be a betrayal of his love for McCone.

There had to be some other way to channel all this rage.

RAE KELLEHER

Alternative Resources had its offices in a six-story smoky-glass building off the 280 freeway in Cupertino. Another not-particularly-attractive monument to the new microchip technology that had sprung from the young and brilliant minds that now populated what had once been an area of orange groves. A quiet revolution had been born here and through booms and busts the world had forever been changed. In 1939, Stanford classmates Bill Hewlett and Dave Packard couldn't have imagined what their tinkering in a Palo Alto garage would lead to.

There was one slot left in the visitors' parking area. Rae squeezed her little BMW into it between two oversize gas-guzzling vehicles. Security was surprisingly lax in the building: the guard at the desk motioned her through without really looking at her credentials. She rode the elevator to the fourth floor and was directed by a receptionist to Cheryl Fitzgerald's office.

Fitzgerald was a plain-faced woman, her skin a doughy white. She wore her graying hair long and parted down the middle; heavy black-framed glasses magnified keen brown eyes. She took time to read Rae's card, then set it on her desk and leaned forward.

"You should have made an appointment, Ms. Kelleher."

"I would have, but I was pressed for time. I'm—"

"I know who you are, who you're married to, the titles of the books you've written, and who you're working for. How is Ms. McCone?"

"Fully cognizant, although she can't move or speak. They call it locked-in syndrome."

"I've read about that. But I hope in her case, the mind triumphs over the body. Are you trying to find out who attacked her?"

"In a way. I'm interested in the Pro Terra Party."

Fitzgerald's face remained impassive, but she removed her glasses and rubbed her eyes. Buying time, Rae thought.

"What on earth would the party have to do with Ms. McCone's shooting?"

"Most likely nothing. It's only one line in the overall investigation."

Such an explanation wouldn't have satisfied Rae, but Fitzgerald accepted it. "What do you want to know?" she asked.

"Why did Don Beckman leave the party?"

"He and I were . . . involved. Pro Terra was our child. But then he decided he wanted a child of our own; I couldn't bring one into the world—not *this* world."

"So he left the party, and you . . . ?"

"Carried on. Until the leadership was co-opted by elements that were at odds with our original philosophy. At that point, I had to resign."

"Who were these elements?"

She hesitated. "I haven't talked about this since I left the party. I was determined to put it behind me and simply lead a useful life. And if I tell you what I know and it becomes public, I'll be up against some very powerful forces. Dangerous people."

"What you tell me will remain confidential." Unless the police made her give it up—but Fitzgerald didn't have to know that.

Fitzgerald glanced at her watch. "It's too long a story, and I have an appointment in five minutes. Why don't you meet me at eleven? There's a coffee shop on the ground floor of the building—the Real Bean. We'll talk then."

Rae waited at a table in the Real Bean, a cooling cup of cappuccino in front of her. Every now and then she'd take a sip, which only reminded her how much she hated designer coffees. Why had she ordered it? Maybe it went with the territory.

All around her casually dressed workers were sipping exotic brews and nibbling on muffins, carrot cake, or sandwiches with an inordinate amount of alfalfa sprouts protruding from them. Many worked on laptops, others read newspapers. Although it was a small shop, none of the patrons acknowledged the others and it seemed to Rae they even avoided eye contact with the counterpersons. Another sign of twenty-first-century isolationism.

Rae watched the clock behind the counter. Eleven-thirteen. Eleven-twenty-two. Eleven-forty. Fitzgerald had been held up at the office . . . she hoped.

Eleven-fifty.

Noon.

Twelve-oh-seven.

No, Rae had been stood up. She left the café, took the elevator to the fourth floor, and asked the receptionist if Ms. Fitzgerald was still in.

"I'm sorry, she isn't."

"When did she leave?"

"At about a quarter to eleven. She said she'd be gone the rest of the day, on urgent personal business. Would you like to make an appointment for tomorrow?"

"No, thank you."

Rae turned away, went to push the elevator button.

Urgent personal business? Was Fitzgerald covering her ass with the "powerful forces" and "dangerous people"?

SHARON McCONE

Last night I dreamed I was flying. It felt so real—the freedom, the soaring, the thrilling turbulence. But then I woke to dull light and immobility, and Hy was gone from the armchair. And I remembered his side of the conversation with Len Weathers that I'd overheard. Became afraid for him all over again.

In my presence, Hy's demeanor had been calm, supportive, and loving. But I felt the tension and rage that was roiling inside him. He would do what he felt he had to do about the person who had put me into this state, even if it forced him to sacrifice himself.

No way to stop this thing he'd set in motion. Unless . . .

Unless I could identify the perp myself—in cooperation with my operatives, of course. Could I guide them in this investigation? Sure. I'd already taken control, my eyes telling them what to do. I'd lead them to the shooter; then they could go to the police and have the person taken into custody where Len Weathers couldn't get at him.

I didn't care what happened to the shooter; if I weren't bound to this bed and could nail him myself, I wouldn't treat him gently. But I didn't want Hy involved in a murder-for-hire case.

Murder for hire.

No, that wasn't Hy's style. He'd told Weathers he needed him if there was a problem. Backup, that was all. Hy would do the job himself. And that would add to the burden of guilt he carried from his time in Southeast Asia—a burden that only in recent years had begun to ease.

Can't let that happen.

I began focusing in a way I never had before: split my energy between trying to will my fingers and toes to move and examining the facts of the case. One finger, one fact. One toe, another fact. Over and over. And the energy, instead of weakening from the split, grew stronger. My mind seemed to expand, to grow—

Although I only imagined the twinge of feeling in my right hand, it gave me hope.

A woman came into my room: short, blonde, with an upturned nose—what in my cheerleading days we used to call perky. She sat in the armchair and introduced herself. Sarah Lawson, speech therapist.

"I understand you're able to communicate yes and no with eyeblinks," she said.

I blinked once.

"That's wonderful, because this afternoon I'm going to start working with you, so you can spell out words with your eyes. One blink, A; two blinks, B; and so on."

And twenty-six blinks, Z. An exhausting process.

"I know what you're thinking," Sarah said, "and I won't deny it. The process is tough, and it'll take a long time until you can put a coherent sentence together. But you can do it; many patients have. A French editor, Jean-Dominique Bauby, dictated an entire book that way."

I'd heard of Bauby. He died within two years of the stroke that disabled him.

I closed my eyes and let the tears flow.

JULIA RAFAEL

By noon, when the SFPD still had no leads on the Haven Dietz murder, Julia decided to drive to the Brandt Institute and share both the Dietz and the Peeples files with Shar.

Shar looked tired, and Julia understood why: on the way in she'd seen Hy escorting Kay Hunt, Shar's adoptive mother, out to his car. Julia had met Mrs. Hunt only once when she'd paid a visit to the pier on one of her trips to the city; she'd seemed fine then, but Julia had heard about the scene here yesterday. Today must have brought more of the same.

Madres! Mierda!

She read each file through verbatim to Shar, held up the photographs appended to them for her to see: formal headshot of Dietz before the attack; group shot with the staff at the financial management firm where she'd been employed; informal and badly lighted snap of her in front of her apartment. Formal shot of Peeples; Larry with his parents at the vineyard; Larry and Ben Gold with Seal Rock in the background. Shar's eyes lingered on all of them.

Julia asked, "Is there something I should be looking into more deeply?"

Blink.

"Peeples?"

Blink.

"The money?"

Blink.

"It had to come from someplace, right? Maybe Thelia or Diane can help me there?"

Blink.

"What about Dietz?"

Blink.

"The police're investigating her murder. You think I should conduct my own investigation?"

Blink, blink.

"What, then? Dig deeper into her background? Maybe go back a long time before she was attacked?"

Blink.

Julia paused, then realized what Shar was trying to tell her. "In her job Dietz had access to a lot of money."

Blink.

"I hear you."

Even if you can't speak, I hear you loud and clear.

CRAIG MORLAND

He and Mick sat across the round table in the conference room, going over the city hall investigation file with Diane D'Angelo. D'Angelo, the latest addition to the agency staff, was tall, willowy, and blonde, with what Craig thought of as patrician features—the kind of woman he'd dated in prep school and college and later in Washington, DC. The kind of woman his parents had expected him to marry.

Sorry, folks. The instant I connected with Adah, I knew why I'd never been serious about any of those well-bred beauties.

He didn't actively dislike D'Angelo, but he couldn't understand why Shar had hired her. She was a poor fit for the agency. Or maybe that *was* why Shar had brought her aboard; the other operatives were an odd mixture, and none of them totally mainstream. Even he, once the standard-issue fed, had been transformed in subtle ways by his relationship with Adah and his move to San Francisco. Maybe Shar's motivation in hiring Diane had been as simple as wanting someone who would blend in at society parties.

Still, Craig didn't completely trust Diane, and he and Mick had decided not to share with her the information about the videos that Craig had found in Harvey Davis's condo.

". . . I didn't think the mayor was all that concerned about the investigation," Diane was saying. "He never spoke to me. Just nodded cordially and went about his business."

"Your only contact"—Mick consulted his notes—"was this aide, Jim Yatz."

"Right. If you're looking for answers—especially to the Teller and Janssen connection—he's the one you should go to."

Mick glanced at Craig and he nodded.

Craig said, "You're hooked into the local scene. What do you know about Yatz?"

Jim Yatz, D'Angelo said, had grown up in the city's Inner Richmond district. His father had been on the board of supervisors for two terms in the early 1970s and held various administrative positions with the city until his death in 2005; he left his son a legacy of public service.

"Jim's father's connections are what got him a scholarship to Georgetown University in DC. He studied public policy, did an internship on Capitol Hill, and then came home." D'Angelo smiled wryly. "This city has a way of luring back those of us who were born here."

Yatz had taken an entry-level job in the city planning commission—a move that surprised those who knew his credentials and political connections. Soon he rose to assistant director, then was tapped by the port commission to look into the demolition or renovation of aging piers. A year ago, the new mayor—a boyhood friend—had hired him as his chief administrative aide.

Jim Yatz was said to be brilliant, politically savvy, and fiercely loyal to the mayor and his administration.

"He's also said to be devious and ruthless if the occasion warrants it," D'Angelo finished.

Craig tapped his pencil on the table, glanced at Mick, who was making a note. "Any personal stuff on Yatz?" he asked.

"Unmarried, dates a lot of beautiful women. Owns a house in the Marina. Entertains lavishly. No," Diane said to Craig's inquiring look, "he's never entertained me. Jim and I . . . well, that goes back a long way."

"To what?"

She shifted her position in her chair, curled a lock of her hair around her index finger—a nervous habit that Craig had previously noted. "He and I . . . we dated when he was in DC and I was in New York. Long-distance relationship, and it didn't work out."

"But he didn't react negatively when we brought you in on the case. In fact, he gave you a strong reference when you applied to work here."

"Jim and I have made our peace. I was the wrong woman for him, but he knew I was the right woman for the job." She frowned. "But it turns out I wasn't."

"Why do you say that?"

"Because if I'd done the job properly, Sharon wouldn't have gotten shot."

"Then let's do the job properly now. You're something of an SF insider. Tell Mick and me what you know about our complicated city government."

RAE KELLEHER

The Summerses' house was up a long, badly paved driveway in the Lafayette hills. Rae maneuvered the low-slung Z4 around the worst of the potholes, but still the undercarriage scraped a couple of times.

Shit! He's a lawyer, they must have money. So why can't they re-pave their own drive?

She parked her car next to a Subaru station wagon in front of the garage and looked up at the house: murky green clapboard made murkier by the shade of the oaks that towered over it; two stories, probably with a third built down the hillside behind. A pretty setting, but a trifle gloomy for her taste.

As she got out of the car a white minivan pulled up behind her, and a slender woman with wavy light brown hair got out and approached her. "Ms. Kelleher? I'm Jane Koziol." They shook hands, and Koziol motioned Rae toward the front door. "Senta's in a pretty bad way, which is why I suggested I meet you here. She wants to hear firsthand about how you found out Alicia was a murder victim. But I'm going to ask you: please spare her the gorier details."

"I didn't bring my file or any crime scene pictures, if that's what you mean. And I'm not into gore myself."

"Good." Koziol rang the doorbell. Its summons was answered immediately by a tall woman with unkempt dark hair that fell to her shoulders; she was wearing a pair of rumpled blue sweats, and the skin around her eyes was red and puffy, her face drawn with sorrow.

Senta Summers greeted them and took them into a living room overlooking an oak grove on the slope below. She asked them to be seated, offered refreshments, which they both declined, then sat tentatively on the edge of the sofa, as if poised for flight.

"You want to know how I found out what happened to your daughter," Rae said.

"Yes. And I want to thank you. The not knowing is what's been so unbearable."

Rae could understand that; the Little Savages weren't even her own children, but if one of them disappeared, she'd've spent many a sleepless night.

Rae provided her with a brief summary of her investigation. "The credit really should go to the Bay Area Victims' Advocates," she added. "They never give up, even when the police do. If you don't mind, would you tell me about Alicia, so I can close out my file properly?"

"I don't know where to begin." Senta made a helpless gesture with both hands.

"What kind of child was she?"

After a long pause, Senta said, "She was a feisty baby who grew into a very willful young adult. At first that seemed a good quality, since she put it to use achieving things: good grades, science fair prizes, an excellent summer job as a counselor at a kayaking camp. She loved to take photographs. That's one of hers over the mantel."

Rae looked where she pointed. A wide-angle view of the sun glinting through the branches of an oak tree. Not professional-quality, but it showed promise.

"She was beautiful and loving," Senta added. "But then it all changed in her senior year."

Alicia, her mother said, had become withdrawn and her grades fell off. She lost her interests, didn't see her friends, and finally began staying away from home for days. "I tried to control her, but she did whatever she wanted. Her father was no help; he told me to back off and give her some space. Then, on July ninth of the year she graduated, she left home for good." Senta Summers paused, shook her head as if to clear it. "All this time I've been hoping she'd come back someday, and now I know she never will."

Jane Koziol took a packet of Kleenex from her purse and passed Senta a tissue.

Rae asked, "Did you file a missing person report?"

"After the requisite seventy-two hours."

"Your husband is politically connected—couldn't he have requested the police look into Alicia's disappearance sooner?"

"My husband prides himself on operating strictly within the law and asks no favors." The words were full of venom.

"What about a private investigator? Did you consider employing one?"

"I wanted to, but Lee said no."

"Why?"

"He was working on an important political campaign, and he was afraid word would get out that we couldn't control our own daughter." Senta's voice was even more bitter.

Time to hit her with the big questions. "Is that why you filed for divorce?"

If she was surprised by Rae's knowledge, she didn't show it. "Among other things. But Lee persuaded me to withdraw the petition in exchange for certain concessions."

"Which were . . . ?"

"I don't see as that's relevant to my daughter's murder, Ms. Kelleher."

Rae glanced at Koziol, then said to Senta, "The things you mention about Alicia—drop in grades, loss of friends and interests— are often signs of depression. And depression in teenagers can often be caused by sexual abuse. Did you ever suspect—?"

"No!" The answer was prompt and loud. "There was nothing like that between Lee and Alicia."

Denial? Or . . . ?

"You're certain?"

"Absolutely. Lee hasn't been able to . . . perform for over ten years. Prostate problems."

"Abuse isn't necessarily defined by penetration."

Senta shook her head emphatically. "There was nothing like that. The truth is, Lee was indifferent to our daughter. Oh, he tolerated her, but only because she was pretty and smart and he could show her off to his political associates. He simply didn't acknowledge her, unless the occasion suited his needs.

"I ask you, do you see him here today? He wasn't here yesterday when I got the news. I waited up till nearly one o'clock to tell him. Then he pretended grief—he's a very good pretender—and gave me a sedative and held me in bed. But at four-thirty in the morning I heard him talking on the phone. And he left at seven, telling me I should arrange for her exhumation from wherever the city buried her so she can be interred in the family plot. Oh, yes, and to call people and plan for a memorial service. God knows what he wants me to tell them she died of."

Rage glinted in Senta's eyes. "I will do all of that, out of respect and love for my daughter. And then I will leave Lee—this time for good."

"His indifference to your daughter—do you have any idea what it stemmed from?"

Senta didn't reply for a moment, looking down at her hands. "Oh, well, what does it matter now? Lee and I were separated at the time Alicia was conceived. We were seeing others, but we also . . . got together a few times. All the same, he thought she wasn't his daughter."

"Was she?"

"I'm not certain. I offered to have a paternity test run, but he wouldn't hear of it. Even though the records would be confidential, he was afraid information would leak out. With Lee, everything is about his reputation."

"So he raised her as his own."

"He gave her everything a child could need or want—except love."

"I'd like to talk with your husband."

"Good luck. Maybe you can catch up with him at Pro Terra Party headquarters. But that's no guarantee he'll give you the time of day—not where his family is concerned."

MICK SAVAGE

He was feeling at loose ends and kind of brain-fogged after his meeting with Craig and Diane, so he took a walk south on the Embarcadero to clear his head. Sat down on one of the granite blocks with the bronze octopus sculptures embedded in it, patting the head of one and staring out over the bay. The day was clear. Runners pounded by on the pavement. Pleasure boats sailed past on the water, probably heading for McCovey Cove by the ballpark; there was a Giants game going on today.

Diane's lecture on city government had bored him. All those special interests fighting each other, all the rivalries and the feuds and the scandals. Didn't anybody think of the common good any more? No—it was me, me, me.

He'd been like that once, a consequence of growing up poor and then having the money gush in when his dad finally made it big in the music business. They'd gone from a tiny rental house to a bigger one that they owned, and then an even bigger one, and finally to a huge estate in the hills above La Jolla. An ancient VW bus was dumped in favor of a Porsche for his dad and a Mercedes for his mom. Other costly cars followed. They shopped constantly; they took trips to exclusive resorts; they built a desert compound south of Tucson, complete with recording studio.

I need, I want, I must have . . .

No longer his philosophy. The irony being that he and Derek were about to get rich off this new software they'd developed.

Rich didn't mean happy, though. Not even contented. He'd seen that in the decline and explosive end of his parents' marriage. Thank God they'd both found other people to love and made peace between themselves.

Okay, enough of that, he told himself. Concentrate on the case.

Sex tapes involving city and state officials. Three murders. Missing document signed only hours before the killings. Exchange of money between Janssen and Teller implied. Other documents missing from city hall. No telling how many highly placed officials were involved in this mess. . . .

The voice on Craig's audiotape of what Janssen had said to Teller at the lodge: "You think you've pulled off a big coup, but these people are dangerous. Consider what they did to Harvey."

What people?

Mick stared out at a sailboat on the bay. Rubbed the bronze octopus head for luck, and stood up.

Time to talk with Shar.

SHARON McCONE

Hy seemed cheerful when he came into my room and plunked an orchid plant on the roll-away table. Yellow flowers. Pretty. Was he planning to replace the weekly roses with orchids, run the gamut from yellow to deep, dark red again?

Or is the transition to yellow a sign that his love's weakening, now that he's saddled with a silent, motionless mummy of a wife?

Don't go there, McCone. You're only entertaining such ideas because you're feeling lousy today.

He kissed me, chased the bad notion away for a while. Flopped in the chair, looking pleased with himself.

"I went over that file about the work you did last year for Amanda Teller again. Deep background on a Cheryl Fitzgerald and a Don Beckman. Founders of the Pro Terra Party, which put Paul Janssen in the state house of representatives."

I wanted to blink, but weariness overcame me. Something wrong, a new low point. Today everything felt negative. Was negative. My breathing wasn't right and my head hurt. Why didn't Hy notice?

He added, "I sense connections, but I can't quite put them together."

I drew a labored breath, shut my eyes.

"What I want to do is call a staff meeting first thing tomorrow morning. Here. I've already cleared it with Saxnay. Is it okay with you?"

With an effort, I opened my eyes, then blinked.

"Great. I'll get Ted started on setting it up."

Why don't you notice something's wrong with me, Ripinsky?

And what else are you getting started on? What about this deal with Len Weathers?

God, there had to be some way to communicate with the man! Tell him how bad I felt. Tell him to change course where Weathers was concerned.

But I was so tired.

I closed my eyes.

"We're going to beat this, McCone. I know we are."

Maybe not.

JULIA RAFAEL

Shar had told her to dig, so she did. Also asked Thelia and Diane to help her.

More background on Haven Dietz. Nothing there she didn't already know. Phone calls to Dietz's former friends and colleagues. Most of them weren't available. She left messages, doubting her calls would be returned.

Julia found she was retracing old ground, repeating things she'd done in the early stages of her investigation. The report Thelia gave her on Dietz's finances was identical to one already on file: Dietz was living on disability payments; she had few assets. Nothing was forthcoming from Diane.

Dios, maybe she wasn't cut out for this kind of work after all. She couldn't get an original angle on the case. She felt like the driver of a car stuck in sand who kept accelerating and digging it in deeper. That wasn't the kind of digging Shar wanted her to do.

She went to the conference room where the coffeepot was. About half a cup left—dark and yucky-looking. She poured it into a mug anyway. While she was there, trying not to choke on the strong brew, Ted stuck his head through the door.

"I can make more of that, if you like."

"No, thanks. Ted, you've known Shar a long time. Has she ever been stuck on a case? So stuck that she never solved it?"

"Not exactly, but . . ." He came all the way into the room, the fluorescents highlighting the gray streaks in his black hair and goatee, and leaned on the edge of the table.

"Her first case for All Souls—a missing person investigation—was a bust. She just couldn't find the guy. Then years later, on the day we moved to the pier, she was going through some boxes of her old papers, and found this last open file. So she read it, noticed something she hadn't before, found the guy, and closed the case."

"She never gives up, does she?"

"No. You shouldn't either."

"How'd you know I was thinking of giving up?"

Ted leaned toward her and patted her cheek. "Because, my dear, I am the Grand Poobah."

Julia went back to her office and started plowing through the Dietz file again. She was halfway through when her phone rang.

"Ms. Rafael, this is Gloria Wickens. You called me earlier about Haven Dietz."

Gloria Wickens—she'd held a higher position than Dietz's at the financial management firm. "Yes. I'm reinterviewing people I spoke with earlier—"

"Well, I'm glad you called. I didn't want to bring this up when I talked with you the last time because I didn't think it was fair to Haven. But I saw in the paper that she was killed, and that makes a difference."

Julia sat up straighter, reached for a pencil and legal pad. "Go on, please."

"The audit of our firm's accounts the year Haven was attacked turned up a shortfall of a hundred thousand dollars. This was ten months after she left the firm."

It was the critical piece of information that might put everything together. "Did they suspect her?"

"I never heard anything to that effect. Another woman, Delia Piper, was under investigation, but eventually exonerated."

"Is Ms. Piper still with the firm?"

"No. She quit, and I heard she moved to Hawaii."

"And nobody ever questioned Ms. Dietz?"

"Why would they? She'd been gone a long time and besides, she was a trust-fund baby. A hundred thousand dollars must've been insignificant to her."

Julia questioned the woman more, but received little additional information. After she ended the call, she thought about her conversations with Dietz: how her parents couldn't help her after the attack because they were sailing across the Pacific in their "damn yacht."

Okay, she'd do an in-depth check on the elder Dietzes.

It showed the yacht had gone down in a storm near Fiji with both of them aboard a year before their daughter was attacked; their estate had barely paid final bills and back taxes.

The things people say that you take at face value.

The things you overlook.

Haven Dietz: rich girl who all of a sudden wasn't going to inherit a cent. Had a good job, but wanted more.

So what else, Julia wondered, had she overlooked?

MICK SAVAGE

Mick ran into Hy in the lobby of the Brandt Institute; Hy was in a hurry because he needed to take Mick's grandma to the airport, but he paused long enough to tell Mick about the staff meeting to be held in Shar's room the next morning.

"How *is* Grandma?"

"She carried on again this morning, and Saskia offered to accompany her back to San Diego," Hy said. "It's for the best. These histrionics . . ." He shrugged.

"What about Elwood?"

"He comes and goes. I don't even know where he's staying."

"Well, he's here for Shar."

"Everybody's here for her." Hy paused. "She's not good today."

A prickle of alarm at the base of Mick's spine. "How so?"

"Not responding much. Sleeping, and there's a lot of rapid eye movement. This has happened a couple of times before, and she's always rallied. I've alerted her nurse. See what you think."

Hy left and Mick went to see his aunt.

She lay on her side facing the window. When he came around the bed, he saw that her eyes were dull and unfocused, her face pale and her breathing ragged.

"Shar?"

No eyeblink.

"Shar!"

No response. He ran out to the nurses' station. Melissa, the night nurse, took one look at his face and together they rushed back to the room.

"She's not responding, but her eyes are open," he said.

Melissa moved swiftly to the side of the bed, looked at Shar, and grabbed the wall phone. She spoke urgently to the operator. "Get the Code Team and Dr. Saxnay to Room Three. Stat!"

"What's happening to her?" Mick asked.

"Please step outside."

"But—"

"Please—go!"

Mick left the room but stayed in the corridor close to the door.

Dr. Saxnay, the attending physician who had taken a personal interest in Shar's case and seemed to live at the institute, rushed past him, barely beating the Code Team through the door. Mick followed, stopped just inside. He could hardly breathe.

"Damn," Saxnay muttered after one look at Shar. He grabbed a tube from the crash cart while the team stood by.

"Get the chopper!" he said to Melissa. "She's going to SF General. Now!" Without waiting for a response, he tubed Shar, handed the tube over to one of the team to keep the oxygen moving. "And don't forget to alert the on-call neurosurgeon over there."

Saxnay spotted Mick. "You! Call her husband and have him meet us at the hospital."

Mick was shaking as he stepped outside, but not far enough to be out of earshot. He pulled his cell phone off his belt.

Saxnay muttered, "Bullet must have dislodged, caused more bleeding. That clot's probably growing by the minute, putting more and more pressure on her brain stem."

"What do you think her chances are?" Melissa asked.

"Her best hope is surgery." Saxnay watched the team transfer Shar to a stretcher, cinch her in for transport. "I was afraid it would come to this. Surgery's going to be tricky, but it's that or lose her."

Lose her!

No! That wasn't possible. They couldn't be talking about Shar.

Flapping rotors and the whine of the helicopter's engine. Feet pounding from a rear entrance. Men grabbed the stretcher, pushed past Mick as if he weren't there.

He watched, numb, as they took his aunt away.

SHARON McCONE

*W*hat's happening to me? God, my heart's pounding like it wants to break through my breastbone.

Light. The light's fading, disappearing.

My sight, the only thing I have left . . . going, gone!

My mind . . .

Where is everybody? Where am I?

No sense of space, place, time.

Alone, so alone.

Rising. Falling.

Dark.

Falling.

Oh, bright flash . . . pain . . . roar . . .

Metal grazing my fingertips.

I see it!

No, I can't. My sight's gone. I'm all alone in the dark.

Falling.

The dark.

Falling, falling . . .

Help! Don't let me die!

HY RIPINSKY

He sat in the waiting room at SF General, surrounded by distraught and anxious strangers, but as alone as if he were on a deserted island. He hadn't called anyone; he couldn't have stood the sympathy and the too-early condolences.

A door opened, a tall dark-haired man in scrubs strode in.

"Mr. Ripinsky, I'm Ben Travers. I'll be your wife's surgeon."

"What're her chances?"

"I don't play the odds with people's lives."

"Meaning not good."

"Meaning we don't know."

"What happened? She wasn't good when I left her today, but she hasn't been good a lot of days."

"In all likelihood, the bullet has moved and a blood clot has formed and is causing more severe pressure on her brain stem. We'll have further information when we get the results of the CT scan. In the meantime, we're prepping her for surgery."

Hy felt a wrenching in his chest. He propped his elbows on his knees, put his face into his hands.

Travers's hand touched his shoulder. "I'll be back as soon as we know something."

"Never mind me. Just save my wife."

Mick came through the doors from the parking lot, his eyes wild, hair disheveled.

"Jesus, Hy," Mick said. "Where is everybody?"

"I didn't make any calls."

"I was at the institute when she . . . I saw something was wrong and got the nurse."

Hy nodded.

"You shouldn't be here alone."

"Go away, Mick."

"What?"

"I *need* to be alone."

"I don't understand."

He'd been alone when Julie died, staring off the bluff at the light—dying, too—on Tufa Lake. Left her in the care of her best friend because she didn't know him any more. He'd always felt guilty about that. Maybe it was his punishment to be alone when Shar died.

Mick said, "No one needs to be by himself at a time like this."

Hy just looked at him. It wasn't something you could explain to anyone else.

Mick backed off, probably seeing the anger and desolation in Hy's eyes. "Okay," he said, "I'll go. But I think you're being selfish. I love Shar, too."

"I'll call you as soon as I know something. And please don't call any of the others."

". . . If that's what you want." Mick turned and left.

Want? All he wanted was for Shar to live.

An hour gone.

"She's still in surgery, Mr. Ripinsky."

"What did the CT scan show?"

"You'll have to talk with her doctor."

An hour and a half gone.

Hank Zahn and Anne-Marie Altman came into the waiting room. Two of Shar's and his best friends. Both attorneys, both calm and rational people. If Mick had to tell someone what had happened—and Hy had seen the need in his eyes—they were the best possible choice.

They sat on either side of him, clasped his hands. Hank, lanky with gray curly hair; Anne-Marie, statuesque and blonde. Curious couple: they lived in different flats in the same building. She bordered on the obsessive about housekeeping, and he was more than slothful. Their adopted teenage daughter, Habiba Hamid, divided her time between their places—although she seemed to favor Hank's more offhand attitude toward housekeeping.

Sharon loved all three of them. So did he.

"Mick called you, huh?"

Hank said, "Yes."

"I told him not to."

"Why?" Anne-Marie asked.

Suddenly Hy felt foolish. Why had he thought he should be alone? Penance? Ridiculous. This was not about him or his past misdeeds.

He said, "Let's wait a while, and if there's no news, then we'll call the others."

RAE KELLEHER

She located Lee Summers at the Pro Terra Party's headquarters in a refurbished warehouse south of Market. A fund-raising party was going on, drinks and canapés being served all around.

The man learns his daughter has been murdered and he attends a party? Incredible!

She'd shown the man at the door her credentials, said she was here on official business. He let her in without question and pointed out Summers. In Rae's experience these gatekeepers—usually hired from security firms—were not always the brightest individuals or totally committed to their jobs. She ought to know; she'd worked security for a time. There was the colleague who read only comic books, moving his lips the whole time; the woman who painted her finger- and toenails while the entire building was burglarized; the man who took sleeping pills on the job. Of course, there were smart and conscientious people, too—many students working their way through college, as Rae and Shar had done—but they usually left for better jobs or different careers.

Now Rae watched Summers from across the room: tall, silver-haired, expensively dressed, his posture and gestures hinting at arrogance. He was surrounded by other well-dressed and attractive people who seemed to hang on his every word. Rae accepted a glass of wine from a passing server, a shrimp canapé from another. Fringe benefits.

A woman who had long gray hair and was wearing a poorly fitting black cocktail dress came out of the crowd and went up to Summers, touching his arm; Rae recognized her—Cheryl Fitzgerald. Summers looked down, clearly not pleased to see her there. She went up on tiptoe and spoke into his ear. When she was finished Summers excused himself and ushered her to a door at the rear of the room.

Rae set down her drink and followed.

The door opened into a long corridor with several other doors opening off it. One stood ajar, and voices came from inside. She slipped along the wall until she was within hearing range.

"... Nothing to connect the party with what happened to Sharon McCone."

"This Rae Kelleher told me it was just one of a number of lines of investigation, but if there wasn't something compelling, why did she bother to come see me?"

"Fishing."

"I'm not so sure. I know about Kelleher and McCone and that agency. They're good. If they find out about Alicia and—"

"Don't mention my daughter's name to me!"

"I saw it on the six o'clock news—the body of a hooker killed in a SoMa alley identified as Alicia. Celebrating, Lee?"

"What kind of comment is that?"

"I've heard the rumors about what you did to her. What if Rae Kelleher finds out about them?"

"Is that a threat?"

"Of course not. But for a while now I've been wanting to move on to someplace where the smog isn't as thick as it is in Silicon Valley."

"Don't even think of blackmailing me, Cheryl. Others have tried; they've all regretted it."

"What others? The mayor? Jim Yatz? Or are you talking about Amanda Teller and Paul Janssen?"

"Clearly you're out of your mind—"

Rae's cellular vibrated. She ignored it.

"... Perfectly sane, and my lawyer has a letter in his safe that tells all about Pro Terra. All I have to do is give the word and it goes straight to the authorities. Or if something happens to me—"

"God, you're melodramatic, Cheryl. What do you want? A trip to an expensive fat farm? You could use it, I admit—"

Sound of a slap.

"Jesus! Okay, what *do* you want?"

"Let's begin with a first-class ticket to Rome."

Rae's cell vibrated again. Shit! It might be important. And Cheryl Fitzgerald wasn't going to pack up her life and move to Italy overnight; plenty of time to find out what knowledge she'd used to exert such pressure on Summers. Rae looked around, saw an exit door, and slipped outside. A ways down the alley, she checked the number—an unfamiliar local one—and answered the call.

"Ms. Kelleher, this is Callie O'Leary. My attorney said you want to speak to me about an inheritance."

Delaney had passed along the message to Alicia Summers's— aka Angie Atkins's—friend, probably in exchange for a cut of the fictional money.

"Yes. When can we meet?"

"Tomorrow, at Mr. Delaney's office?"

"I'd rather we do this one-on-one. Your attorney . . ."

Long pause. "Yes, I understand. I'm staying at Hope House in the outer Richmond. It's a shelter for women at risk. I'll give you the address."

"I can be there in less than an hour."

CRAIG MORLAND

Close to eleven. He pushed away from his desk and the voluminous paper files on the city hall investigation. He'd replayed the surveillance tapes he'd made on Teller and Janssen from his room at the Big Sur lodge. They'd run out some time between when he fell asleep and when he was awakened by the shots, but the Monterey County authorities could use what was there.

Now he was having a crisis of conscience. The tapes were illegal. If he turned them over to the sheriff's department, it could compromise his license and the agency. Even sending them anonymously would be a risk. Besides, as a former fed, he harbored a great distrust of local law-enforcement agencies.

Screw them, he thought. He'd probably solve the case before they even broke significant ground.

To that end, he slipped one of the DVDs he'd taken from Harvey Davis's condo into the computer and watched it once again.

A tall, slender woman—naked, her blonde hair cascading over her shoulders. Facing away from the camera. A man, facing her, but in shadow so his features weren't clear.

"Oh, baby, you are something else. As advertised and then some."

"Tell me I'm beautiful. I've always wanted somebody to tell me I'm beautiful."

"You're beautiful. You are beautiful."

Cut to another, similar shot. Different man, different shape, but also in shadow.

"You're worth the money I gave, all of it."

"Because I'm pretty."

"And incredibly hot."

"How much money did you give?"

"A lot."

"I could use some money for myself. They never give me anything. Would you pay that much to me? If I'm good to you?"

"If you're very, very good . . ."

Next scene: a couple in bed, indistinguishable except for the long sweep of blonde hair. Graphic noises.

Next: similar recording.

Craig ejected the DVD, slipped the other one in.

Another unclear view: a man with a hairy back, humping.

Another man, a tattoo visible on his shoulder. The same well-publicized tattoo of the insignia of USC, his alma mater, that the mayor bore in the same place. He'd often joked with the press that he intended to have it removed, since his wife had graduated from rival UCLA.

And now the last one: two unidentifiable naked women, one blonde and one dark-haired, twined in an embrace.

The dark-haired one: Amanda Teller, or someone made up to look like her.

Craig slowed the recording speed, played the disc again.

The mayor's tattoo could have been faked. The woman who resembled Teller could be younger than the dead supervisor.

Where had Harvey Davis gotten these discs? Who had made them? And who were the unidentifiable participants?

Craig checked his watch. After one now, but his friend Daniel Blackstone down in Scottsdale, a video and audio forensics specialist, would probably still be at his computer. Daniel worked best in the cool night, slept best during the hot daylight hours.

Craig punched in his number and got an immediate response.

"You need work?" he asked.

Daniel laughed—a habitually harsh sound exacerbated by the

two packs of Marlboros he smoked daily. "I've got plenty of work, but I can fit you in. What's the job?"

Craig outlined what he thought about the videos.

"That shouldn't be any problem. You want to messenger them to me?"

He thought about the call he'd received earlier from Hy. He wouldn't be doing McCone any good sitting around a hospital waiting room.

"Just a second."

His fingers skipped over the keyboard. Southwest Airlines had a seven a.m. flight that got into Phoenix's Sky Harbor at nine-fifteen. Seats were available.

"I'll see you around ten-thirty tomorrow," he said.

JULIA RAFAEL

Now she was digging deep on the embezzlement at Haven Dietz's former financial management firm. Reviewing the reports Thelia had delivered to her, plus information on the woman, Delia Piper, who had been accused of the crime and then exonerated. Piper now lived in Hawaii, on Oahu: four hours earlier there. Julia got her number from information and called.

"Of course it was Haven," the woman said when Julia had explained about her investigation. "I never doubted it, and neither did a number of my colleagues. The audit couldn't pinpoint the time of the embezzlement, but she was still with the firm the first two months of its fiscal year."

"Why did they suspect you?"

"I had more responsibility than Haven, and access to cash. Also—I admit it—I was the company bitch. A lot of people didn't like my style. Still don't. And I'd been very outspoken about the conduct of our married branch manager, with whom Haven was having an affair."

"Oh? And he is . . . ?"

"Was. Todd Daley. He committed suicide a week after Haven was attacked. Shot himself. I guess he was afraid she would talk."

"I understand Ms. Dietz didn't have access to cash."

"No, but Todd Daley did."

"So you think they were in on the embezzlement together?"

"Well, sure. Todd had a shrewish wife and three snot-nosed

kids in a tract house in Pacifica. Haven was pretty and smart. A hundred thousand dollars doesn't sound like much to start a new life on, but Todd knew how to make money work for the clients. Haven must've persuaded him to let the clients' money work for them."

The venom in Delia Piper's voice annoyed Julia. "Ms. Piper, are you aware that Haven Dietz is dead?"

"No. Really?"

"She was killed by an intruder in her apartment Sunday night."

"Well, that's too bad, but I don't feel sorry for her. The woman was one of the most unpleasant people I ever worked with."

That, coming from the self-described office bitch.

Haven Dietz, her boss Todd Daley, a hundred thousand dollars missing from the management firm but not discovered till the annual audit.

Haven walking through the park on her way home, a small fortune in cash in her briefcase.

Haven brutally attacked, the briefcase gone.

A hundred thousand dollars in the tack room at the Peepleses' vineyard.

Was Larry Peeples Haven's attacker? Had she perhaps confided her plans to him?

But then why had he nursed Dietz back to health?

And why had he abandoned the cash?

And where was he now?

RAE KELLEHER

She'd meant to get to the Hope House an hour after Callie O'Leary's call, but everything had conspired against her. Ticket for making an illegal U turn on the Embarcadero; accident blocking an intersection on Franklin Street; heavy traffic on Geary; and no parking spaces within six blocks of her destination.

Now it was after eleven. Would they even let her in to talk with O'Leary?

The safe house was brick, three stories. Edwardian style. A porch light shone brightly and there was muted light in some of the windows. Rae went up the front steps, noticed the eye of a surveillance camera trained on her as she rang the bell. A female voice came through a speaker above the bell, asking her to identify herself.

She did, holding up her credentials to the camera.

"I'll be right there," the voice said.

A woman dressed in jeans and a sweatshirt opened the door. "Callie's been waiting a long time for you, Ms. Kelleher."

"I realize that. I'm sorry."

"Not my problem. I'd've been up anyway; it's my night on the door. Callie's in the coming-together room." She gestured toward an archway to her right.

Interesting name for living room. Rae liked it.

She went over there and looked in. A dark-haired woman was curled in an oversize armchair, an afghan pulled up to her shoulders. The room was filled with similar comfortable furnishings, and a gas log flickered on the small tiled hearth—a fireplace that had once burned coal, but was later converted.

When Rae cleared her throat, the woman started and looked up. Rae saw that she was a beauty. Big, heavily lashed gray eyes, sculpted chin and cheekbones. But the bleakness in those eyes and the tight lines around her mouth told of a hard life. As did the yellowing bruise on her chin. She couldn't've been much over twenty.

"Ms. O'Leary, I'm Rae Kelleher. Sorry to be so late."

"No worries. I don't sleep much anyway. This story about an inheritance—it's not true, is it?"

"No, it's not. How did you know?"

"I don't have any relatives, at least not any that would leave me money."

"Then why did you call me, agree to meet with me?"

Callie O'Leary motioned for Rae to be seated across from her. "Because this has got to be about Angie. I saw on the news that they identified her body. I know . . . quite a few things about Angie, and it's time I told somebody."

Rae's phone buzzed. She looked at the number, saw it was Hy and said, "I need to take this."

After she'd ended the call, she sat silently for a moment, fingers pressed to her lips, feeling sick inside.

"Bad news?" Callie O'Leary asked.

". . . Yes."

"You need to leave? We can talk another time. I'll be here until it's safe for me to get out of town."

Rae forced her mind away from what Hy had told her about Shar and back to the situation at hand. "No," she said. "It's bad news, but there's nothing I can do to help."

Besides, she was doing what Shar would want her to.

"So how come you're here?" she asked Callie.

"Guy threatened me."

"Don't you get a lot of threats in your line of work?"

"Not like this. Not from somebody so powerful."

"Somebody connected with Angie?"

She nodded.

"Tell me about it."

O'Leary's earlier resolve had faded. "This guy, he'll kill me if I do."

"Not if he can't find you."

"He can find me, a guy like that. And the security isn't all that good here."

"I know a place where it is."

Ricky was going to be amazed when she brought a hooker home.

TUESDAY, JULY 22

HY RIPINSKY

After midnight. Still no word.

Once he'd made his calls people started to arrive. Ted and Neal. Ricky, in lieu of Rae, who was working a lead. Craig had stopped in briefly, but he would be off on an early morning flight tomorrow, pursuing another lead. Julia. Robin Blackhawk, Shar's half sister. Brother John. Mick. And Elwood Farmer, sitting silent and calm by himself. Hy hadn't called Elwood because he assumed the traditional old man didn't have a cell phone, but Ricky had supplied a number. An iPhone, no less. Traditional or not, Elwood had entered the twenty-first century in style.

Two hours gone now, and nothing from the doctor. Two hours in surgery: God, what a toll that must be taking on his wife's weakened body!

He wondered what he'd been thinking, sitting here alone and refusing company. Refusing comfort. Since he'd changed his mind he was surrounded by the most caring people he'd ever known. Family, what a family should be. What they so often weren't.

The nurse on the desk was eyeing them nervously. So many people crowding the waiting room. Hy went up to her and asked, "Do you want some of them to leave? They can sit with me in shifts."

"No, Mr. Ripinsky. They can stay as long as they behave themselves."

"Well, that's kind of a risky proposition. Anybody misbehaves, you tell me and I'll throw them out myself."

He crossed the room to Elwood, sat down beside him. Shar's birth father nodded to him, but remained silent.

Hy felt uncomfortable; he barely knew the man, and even McCone had been struggling to connect with him.

"She will be all right," Elwood said.

Hy glanced at him, startled.

"How do you know that?" he asked.

"*Saika mukua kettae.* Her spirit is strong." Farmer shrugged. "Some things, you just know."

"Because you're her father?"

"Well, there's something about blood." He shot a keen look at Hy. "You know how strong she is. Why are you doubting her?"

He thought on the question. "Maybe because I'm not sure how well I'd do in the same situation."

Elwood made a dismissive motion with his hand. "Then doubt yourself, not your wife."

Doubt himself. He'd been doing that ever since Southeast Asia. Why transfer the feeling to Shar? Elwood was right—just stop the doubting altogether.

"*Saika mukua kettae.*"

After a moment Elwood added, "You can't take control of her physically; the doctors are doing that. But mentally, emotionally . . ." He shrugged again.

"Thanks. I'll try."

They sat there together in silence, waiting for news, and Hy felt the strength that radiated from Shar's father.

Three hours gone.

RAE KELLEHER

Callie O'Leary asked, "You *live* here?"

"I do." They had just pulled through the automatic gate to the house in Sea Cliff; to the north the Golden Gate Bridge shone orange through the gathering mist. The big, multistoried residence loomed before them, soft lights in only a few of its windows.

"Awesome," Callie said, "but where're all the security guys?"

"They're here. You just don't see them—and neither do intruders."

"Rad. This PI business, it must pay real good."

Rae smiled and stopped the car. "It helps to have married well."

They got out and went to the front door, where Rae punched numbers on a keypad, then let them in and rearmed the system. The house was quiet: the younger kids had gone back to Charlene and Vic's home in Bel Air, Chris was at her apartment in Berkeley, and Mick was probably at the hospital. Ricky, too—he'd promised he'd fill in for her.

When they entered the living room, Callie again said, "Awesome!"

"Are you hungry?" Rae asked. "Do you want a drink?"

". . . I'm not hungry and I haven't had a drink since I went to Hope House. Probably I shouldn't now."

"Soda? Coffee? Anything else?"

"No thanks. All I want to do is sit down on that couch and look at that beautiful fireplace. I've never seen one like that, just standing in the middle of the room with rock all around it."

Rae motioned for Callie to sit. "Where're you from?" she asked.

"You mean where I was born? Honolulu. My dad was in the navy. We moved a lot. I headed out when they were gonna leave San Diego for someplace on the East Coast."

"Why?"

"Why not? I had three brothers. They liked them better than me. And I liked San Diego." She looked sharply at Rae. "And no, nobody abused me. They . . . just didn't care if I was there or not."

"So you were living in San Diego . . . ?"

"And a guy made me an offer I couldn't refuse. Move to LA, live in his penthouse, make a lot of money. Old stupid story, and I don't want to talk about it."

"That's cool."

The front door opened. "Hey, Red, where are you?" Ricky, back from the hospital.

"Living room."

She could hear him pulling off his coat and hanging it on the rack in the entryway. He called, "Shar's still in surgery. They were getting edgy about a cast of thousands in the waiting room, so I took a break."

He appeared in the archway, and his gaze rested on Callie. "Hi. Who's this?"

"A new friend, Callie O'Leary."

Something flickered in his eyes; he knew exactly what she was. He'd had plenty of contact with women like her in the music business.

"Well, Callie," he said, "welcome to our home."

Callie's eyes widened and she turned to Rae. "Oh my God, you *did* marry well. Ricky Savage! I can't believe it! I've listened and listened to his music hundreds of times, and I saw that movie he did last year."

"Crappy movie," Ricky told her. "But I thought I looked okay in a beard."

Rae said, "Callie needs a safe place to stay. And she wants to tell me something."

He replied, "A safe place is what we have to offer."

HY RIPINSKY

Four and three-quarters hours gone.

He grasped Ted's hand, thought about praying.

Funny thought, for an atheist.

Religion just didn't work for him. What worked was the life force: McCone, loving her, soaring through the sky together. . . .

He concentrated on that.

A man in blood-spattered green scrubs entered the waiting room. At first glance Hy didn't recognize him, then he realized he was Dr. Ben Travers, the surgeon with whom he'd briefly spoken before Shar went into surgery.

The blood—his wife's.

He stared at the doctor, trying to read his face. It looked like a mask.

Ted let go of Hy's hand, motioned that he should stand up.

He did, and moved toward the surgeon, hoping for the best, steeling himself for the worst.

CRAIG MORLAND

He always got lost in Scottsdale.

It was strange, because he had a good sense of direction and the city was laid out on a grid. But there were a few twists and turns that he couldn't comprehend, and although Daniel Blackstone's house was on Mariposa Street close to the main shopping area, Craig kept taking side streets and passing the same roundabout with the rearing life-size bronze horses in its center. The third time past, he called Daniel.

"Not again," his friend said. "Don't you have GPS?"

"On this piece of shit rental? Give me a break—and directions."

"Where are you?"

"By the horses."

"Coming from which way?"

"How the hell should I know?"

A sigh. "Take the street—I forget its name—where there's a gallery on one side and a jeweler's on the other."

"All you have in this town is jewelry stores and galleries."

"It's right there, past the horses."

"North or south?"

Another sigh. "West."

"Which way is west?"

"Just look for the sun and go the other way. Then turn left on my street."

"Yes, boss."

Craig and Daniel Blackstone had been friends during their FBI years in DC. Had pub-crawled and trolled for women together, gone to ball games, spent time gambling in Atlantic City. Then Daniel had split from the Bureau—something to do with one of his cases that involved a political cover-up that he would never talk about—and a couple of years later Craig had gone to San Francisco to be with Adah. They'd stayed in touch, though, and more than once he'd tapped into Daniel's expertise.

He made the left turn and finally spotted the house—nondescript beige stucco, surrounded by pink and white oleanders and palm trees. Craig parked at the curb, got out of the small rental car, and stretched his cramped muscles. The house's door opened and Daniel's voice called, "You find the place all right?"

"Asshole," Craig muttered.

"Say that louder."

"Asshole!"

Daniel Blackstone was tall and lean, with chiseled features and long dark hair secured in a ponytail. He wore turquoise rings and the buckle of the belt that cinched his jeans was one that he'd told Craig he'd bought from a down-and-out rodeo champion. A Western shirt and string tie completed his outfit.

Daniel was from Maryland, but he'd gone native in Arizona.

"You want a beer?" he asked, heading back toward the kitchen.

"A beer? Man, it's the middle of the morning."

"I don't keep local hours. As they say, the sun's over the yardarm—someplace."

Well, why not?

"I got chips and guacamole, too."

Even better.

A few minutes later Craig was seated in a deep armchair in Daniel's office—beer, chips, and guac to hand and computers and audio equipment all around. Daniel was working at one of the monitors, ashes from his cigarette falling onto the keyboard.

After a moment he said, "It's the same young blonde woman in every scene. Voiceprint is identical."

"Can you tell anything about her?"

"Well educated. Has that overprivileged lilt—you know, the one that makes factual sentences into a question. Like that one you were so hung up on in DC—what was her name?"

"Can't remember."

"Oh, yeah—Lauren. Lovely Lauren. You took her away from me."

"You never had her to begin with."

"Valid point." Daniel paused. "All right, I'm doing a high-res zoom on the guy with the tattoo. You think it's SF's mayor?"

"Could be."

"Not. This tattoo is a press-on. Come over, look at it."

Craig got up and looked over Daniel's right shoulder. Daniel zoomed in ever closer. "See this edge? It's tipped up a little. And the skin tone's different, filtered through the latex."

"So it was a setup."

"Right. Now watch this." He clicked on another scene—the woman and the Amanda Teller lookalike. "It's a good fake, judging from the photos of Teller you've given me, but there's one little problem: check out her skin."

Craig squinted at the magnified image. "What about it?"

"Teller was in her forties. This woman is in her early twenties."

"I'll take your word for it. Can you get clearer images of the men in the scenes with the blonde woman?"

Daniel looked over his shoulder and smiled at him. "I don't like to talk about bears shitting in the woods, but . . ."

HY RIPINSKY

So damn many hours gone that he didn't try to count them any more.

McCone had survived the surgery. They'd removed the clot and the bullet and bone fragments and God knew whatever else crap from her skull.

But now the waiting began.

The next several hours were critical, Travers had said.

Hy sat next to Elwood, who hadn't stirred except for the occasional cigarette break outside. Hadn't spoken much either. The others had come and gone, as if in orchestrated shifts. They chattered and tried to cheer him, but he preferred Elwood's silence.

It was after noon when Travers came out and told him for the third time that the next few hours were critical.

His fists clenched. He felt like leaping on the doctor, demanding reassurance.

Elwood's weathered, long-fingered artist's hand touched his. "She will survive, but first *tsa'niigh saika bennenda'ga*. Loosely translated, that means let her go."

"Let her go? That's insane!"

"Set her free. She'll come back to you."

"What's that, some fuckin' Indian mysticism?"

Elwood released Hy's hand. Smiled.

"No, it's simple wisdom. Before this is over, you'll own a large share of it yourself."

JULIA RAFAEL

She'd been up all night. Her eyes felt gritty and her head throbbed. Several hours at the hospital, then home, where Tonio was sick with some kind of stomach flu and she'd taken over so Sophia could get some sleep. Then to the hospital, and back to the pier after she'd found out Shar had survived the surgery.

Dios gracias!

Thelia's reports—nothing from Diane—only contained information she already had. So she got on the computer and read through old newspaper accounts of Haven Dietz's attack and the embezzlement at her brokerage firm. Looking for that shred of information that might provide a lead.

Nothing.

She pushed away from the monitor, picked up the phone, and called Hy at the hospital. No change in Shar's condition; still waiting.

How could he stand it, when she could barely stand it herself? If only she'd gone back to the pier with Shar that night after they'd had dinner. If only she'd told her retrieving the cell phone could wait, invited her over for a glass of wine. If only Shar wasn't so forgetful about gassing up her car.

All the if-onlys, and focusing on them didn't change a thing.

She closed her eyes, leaned back in her chair, and thought about Haven Dietz. Leaving the brokerage firm with a hundred thousand dollars in her briefcase. Walking across the park from her bus. The briefcase had been found empty in a trash can several yards from where she was attacked—a scarred black leather case that had seen better days. Not a case that would attract a thief.

Someone had known the contents of that case.

And he or she had come prepared to carry the cash away, probably in the duffel bag that had been stashed under the floorboards of the Peepleses' tack room.

The attack had been savage. Dietz's assailant had taken out extreme rage and hatred on her.

Larry Peeples?

Julia couldn't stand sitting around, waiting on word about Shar, waiting for a sudden inspiration to strike her. She looked at her watch: eleven o'clock, a good time for a drive to the wine country.

RAE KELLEHER

She'd stayed up late questioning Callie, slept a few hours. When she got up she made arrangements for the woman to give a deposition to Ricky's and her attorney, then fly to New York City and stay at an apartment that Zenith Records, Ricky's company, maintained there. An associate of Ricky's would keep tabs on Callie until legal action about the things she had told Rae could be set in motion.

Rae checked with the hospital—Shar was hanging in there but far from out of the woods. She cooked Callie breakfast, then took her to the attorney's office and then the airport. When she got back home, she listened to the tapes she'd made of their conversation. The only detail Callie had been reticent about was who had threatened her, but Rae could guess.

". . . Lee Summers pimped his own daughter. At first it was like, she was pretty so he'd take her around, show her off to political people. But then he was setting her up with guys he wanted to give him a donation or owe him favors. . . . I don't know who, but they were important.

"She told me she freaked the first time, didn't know her dad had turned her over to this older guy for sex. But after a while she kind of got into it, because it was a way of sticking it to Daddy in return. I could've told her Daddy couldn't care less, but she didn't want to hear it. He's one cold son of a bitch, that Summers. . . .

"I met her when Summers hired me to do a twosome with her. She was pretty drugged up, didn't even know they were video-taping it. Afterwards I took her home with me, sobered her up, calmed her down. She didn't want to go back to her parents' place, so I let her stay. She changed her name, bought fake ID, turned some tricks, and six weeks later she was dead. . . .

"Yeah, I knew who she really was, but I wasn't gonna go to the cops with it. That Lee Summers is a bad dude; I wouldn't be surprised if he killed her himself. . . . Why? Because she was outside of his control. What if she decided to go to the press? What if she told somebody and they talked?

". . . I don't know who else was involved in the taping. Summers hired me, and a director and a couple of porn techies that I've seen around town handled the shoot. . . . No, I can't give you their names, but they work for a production company, Hot Shots. They've got an office and soundstage on Howard Street.

". . . I'm talking to you because I read about what happened to your boss and I think Lee Summers had a hand in it. I hate men like him. I think you might be able to do something about this; then I won't have to be looking over my shoulder my whole life."

Rae clicked off the recorder.

All right, she thought, *on to Hot Shots.*

MICK SAVAGE

He'd been at the hospital for hours, but there was no change in Shar's condition and he needed to do something at the pier. It was nearly noon, when Diane D'Angelo always left promptly for lunch—a good time for him to get into her files on the city hall case.

Craig distrusted the socialite who was playing at being an investigator, and Mick did, too. Not only because she'd produced no results on the case, but because her self-blaming remark about how Shar had gotten shot because she'd failed to solve the case smacked of insincerity, and—he'd realized this afternoon—the woman had never once visited his aunt since she'd been hospitalized. Everybody else from the agency had been at both SFG and the Brandt Institute.

Mick parked his Harley in his allotted space on the pier's floor. Of the vehicles belonging to agency personnel, only Ted's new red Smart car was there. He went upstairs, looked into Ted's office: the office manager—or Grand Poobah, as he jokingly referred to himself—was at his desk, scowling at the computer monitor. Mick slipped by unobserved.

The agency's system was difficult for outsiders to access, but simple for employees. They were a team, they trusted each other, no need to take extra precautions. Mick pulled his chair up to his workstation and began typing in passwords.

Diane D'Angelo's files were blocked.

Uh-huh, but not for long. Not with the new software he and Derek had developed for just such contingencies.

He accessed the blocked files within three minutes. Found the ones D'Angelo had passed along to Craig and him, and also the file on the inquiry that Shar had handled last year for Amanda Teller. The one Derek had retrieved for Hy on Monday.

No reason for D'Angelo to have that file.

Next job: find out about the woman.

Mick's fingers tapped over the keyboard as he moved from one search engine to another. What he discovered didn't surprise him.

She wasn't who she claimed to be. Diane D'Angelo, formerly of San Francisco and then of New York City, had died in a boating accident off the coast of Maine five years ago.

So who was this imposter? And why hadn't Shar run a routine background check when she hired her? Or asked Derek or him to do it?

He began searching again.

JULIA RAFAEL

She arrived at the Peepleses' winery at a quarter to one. It was hot in the Valley of the Moon, the surrounding vineyards still on this windless day. A couple of men in work clothes and sunshade hats were out, doing whatever people did to tend vines, but they moved in slow motion. Julia parked in the driveway and went down a path at the side of the house to the stables, where Judy Peeples had told her she'd be. The tall, frail woman was grooming a big black horse that, to Julia, looked mean and dangerous.

When she called out, Mrs. Peeples turned and greeted her. She set down the brush she'd been using on the horse and put him in his stall, then came over and shook Julia's hand.

"I'm sorry my husband can't be here," she said. "He's at a winemakers' luncheon in town. A regular monthly event. I didn't want him to miss it; he's had so little diversion since he discovered that money."

"And you? How're you holding up?"

"Oh . . ." She made a dismissive gesture. "I have my diversions. I ride and I consult with our accounting personnel and I look after Thomas."

And who looks after you?

Julia bit back the question, asked, "Could I take another look at the money and the bag that it was in?"

"Oh, dear. You came all the way up here for that?"

"Yes. Is there a problem?"

"Well, the money is still in the safe, but the bag—Thomas disposed of it."

"Why? It was evidence!"

"Evidence of our son's wrongdoing, Thomas said. He didn't want it in the house."

"*Mierda!*"

Mrs. Peeples looked conflicted. After several seconds she said, "It's true that the bag isn't in the house any more. But I removed it from the trash and put it back where he found it, under the floor of the tack room. It's evidence, but I don't care what my son did. I just want to know what happened to him."

They went into the tack room and Julia pried up the floorboard. The bag was newish black leather with a plaid lining. No initials, nothing distinctive.

"Mrs. Peeples, had you ever seen this bag before your husband found it?"

"No, never."

"Has he?"

"I don't think so." But doubt flickered in her eyes, indicating the opposite.

"Can I take it with me? A laboratory my agency uses might be able to tell me more about it."

"Please, take it. I want it out of here. It's been on my conscience, going against my husband's wishes."

Julia drove back to the city, the duffel bag a silent passenger beside her.

RAE KELLEHER

ot Shots was located in a former auto-body shop on Howard
Street near the Highway 101 on-ramp. Its facade still bore
the weathered name—Don's Fix It—but the overhead doors had
been boarded up. A small entry opened off the space between the
building and the one adjacent to the south. It was blocked by a
grille, an intercom beside it.

On the way Rae had debated what approach would most likely get
the people there to volunteer information. She put the one she'd decided on into operation as soon as a male voice responded to her ring.

"Hi, I'm Rae Kelleher. My husband, Ricky Savage, and his part-
ners own Zenith Records."

"Yes?" the voice said.

"We've seen some of your films, and we're interested in speaking with one of the directors."

"Wait a minute—Zenith Records. What's that got to do with
our films?"

"We're diversifying. Are you interested?"

Long pause. "Call back tomorrow."

"Onetime offer. Are you interested?"

". . . Come on in."

"Nick Carson," the slender, trendily dressed man said, holding out
his hand. He looked like an Internet entrepreneur, not a porn-flick
maker.

She shook the hand. "Rae Kelleher."

"We can talk in my office." He motioned to a short hallway.

Rae looked around. A pair of closed doors, red lights burning above them.

"Shooting today?"

"Yes." Tersely.

Carson led her down the hallway to an office that might have housed a busy accountant—spreadsheets on the desk, an adding machine, a computer. The computer was on, but Carson blocked her view of it and closed the file displayed there. He motioned toward a straight-backed chair, sat in an upholstered one behind the desk. Eyed her keenly. His eyes were blue, his features regular, his dark hair slicked back into a short ponytail.

"So Zenith Records wants to go into the porn business," he said.

"Not exactly. We're interested in the film industry—as I said, one of your directors."

"His name?"

"I don't know. He did some work for the Pro Terra Party."

Understanding came into Carson's eyes. "And you and Mr. Savage just happened to see his work where?"

"Pirated copies of DVDs that a friend loaned us. We're . . . into that sort of thing."

"Like to watch, do you?"

"Well, yeah."

"And what makes this director so special?"

Rae shrugged. "I don't know. My husband asked me to find out who he was."

"I see. Why didn't he do it himself?" There was a silver letter opener on the desk; Carson toyed with it.

"I'm better than my husband at locating people."

"You know what? I don't believe your story."

"Why not?"

"Zenith Records is not going into film. You're interested in this director because you want to make your own film. You like to watch, so why not watch yourselves? Right?"

"Okay, you've caught me out. So can you put me in touch with him?"

"Yes, I can. But she's a woman—Laura Logan. I'll call her, ask her to get in touch with you." His smile showed small, pointed teeth. "That way she'll be sure to give me the twenty percent I get for throwing jobs her way."

CRAIG MORLAND

By two-fifty he was airborne again. Going back to SF with a briefcase full of photos and enough information to shake city and state government to its foundations.

After takeoff, he tilted his seat back and thought about the prints Daniel had made for him from the videos.

The woman with the long blonde hair: no clue as to her identity.

The same for the dark-haired woman in bed with her.

But the men: top city hall figures and state officials, including Jim Yatz, the mayor's closest associate.

Craig looked out the window at Phoenix's receding smog-shrouded skyline, making connections.

Okay, somebody was trying to gain control over the city hall crowd, as well as minor state officials. They couldn't entice the mayor or Amanda Teller, so they did their best to fake it.

Teller had had a hold over State Representative Paul Janssen. Forced him to sign a document.

Their deaths had been arranged to look like a murder-suicide pact, and someone had taken the document.

So how did all of this pertain to the attack on Shar?

Still unclear.

He thought of the call he'd received from Mick before he boarded his flight: "We've got an imposter in the office. Diane

D'Angelo is really Susan Angelo, a small-time investigator from DC—and a close friend of Jim Yatz."

So Yatz had probably hired her to find out what was in the agency files about the city hall investigation. But she had free run of the office and its computer system. Why would she have gone there at night to retrieve information and end up shooting Shar?

Whatever, Diane and Yatz were dirty, and they were going down. A large number of state and city officials as well. And the mayor, whom Craig liked, would have a hell of a time extricating himself from this one.

No worries. He'd done it before. The mayor was one slick, smart bastard.

HY RIPINSKY

It was after four in the afternoon when Ben Travers came out and told him the news—the *good* news. McCone was awake and responsive—not locked in any more. He could see her briefly.

"Don't expect too much," Travers told him as they took the elevator to intensive care. "We don't yet know what damage the pressure on her brain stem did. Even if it's not severe, she's still got a long way to go—therapy, relearning skills she's lost."

"But she'll be all right?"

"Ultimately that's what we're hoping for. The important thing is that she's alive and cognizant."

Hy leaned heavily against the elevator wall. "I don't care how long it takes for her to recover. Just so she does."

Travers looked as if he wanted to say more, but the elevator door opened. He led Hy through a large circular area of rooms arranged around a central nurses' station. Each room had a window and its door was open—so the nurses could monitor the patients from the desk, Hy supposed.

Shar's head was swathed in bandages and she was hooked up to monitors that kept blinking on and off, providing running strips of information. Her eyes were open, and they lighted up when she saw him.

Hy kissed her cheek. "Welcome back. You'll be all the way back in time."

Doubtful look.

"Don't try to talk now. You need your rest."

Hy studied her face. The skin below her eyes looked bruised and her complexion was sallow. There were lines around her mouth that he hadn't noticed before. But she was alive, and that was everything to him—everything.

She regarded him with a long, intense stare.

"They removed a blood clot and some bone and bullet fragments. No more pressure on your brain stem now."

Still she stared at him.

"Dr. Travers, your surgeon, will explain more fully later on."

Still staring.

"You want to know about the investigation. Is that it?"

Blink.

"You're insatiable."

He explained that everybody was working 24/7, gathering data. Once they had all they could get, they'd pool their information and present it to her. Another eyeblink. Then her lids closed and stayed that way.

Hy kissed her again and slipped out of the room. In the corridor he faltered and steadied himself on a railing. The constant emotional highs and lows had left him exhausted—but he wasn't ready to give in to it yet. He'd go back to the waiting room and talk with Elwood. Then he'd begin to make phone calls.

"Now you realize her strength, Son."

Nobody had called him "Son" since his daddy tangled with those high-tension wires in his beat-up old crop duster. He guessed he'd qualified as family with Elwood.

"Oh, Hy! My baby's all right! Did you hear that, Saskia—our baby's all right!"

Kay started wailing. Why the hell hadn't Saskia or Melvin answered the phone?

"You know what I'm gonna do tonight? Clean this house. We can't have Shar coming home to a dirty place."

Well, maybe John would finally get rid of the empty beer bottles.

"You've reached Charlene and Vic . . ."

"Patsy and Evans are heading for the Bay Area. If this is about restaurant business, please call 801-2345 and speak with Nora."

"Rae Kelleher. Please leave a message."

"This is Julia Rafael. I'm sorry I can't answer the phone . . ."

"This is Ann-Marie. I'm not available . . ."

"Hank Zahn here. Leave a message, and I'll get back to you."

Dammit, people had cell phones so they could keep connected. Then they turned them off at a critical moment.

"McCone Investigations, Ted Smalley speaking."

Finally—a real voice again.

"It's Hy. Shar's awake, not locked in any more. They think she'll eventually be okay."

"I knew it! I just knew it!"

"I've been trying to tell everybody, but most've them are unavailable. Is anybody else there?"

"Craig and Mick are, and if you can leave Shar, I think you ought to get over here. Something ugly's about to go down."

SHARON McCONE

I'm still alive! And I'm not going to be a vegetable after all. Just days ago, the future looked so bleak, but now . . .

Tears again. One thing that hadn't changed was the roller-coaster ride of emotions.

I could see nurses moving around hurriedly, checking on other patients, carrying medicines. No downtime on the floor of an ICU. Nurses—I'd never before had so much respect for individuals in any single profession. Well, except for doctors or cops or firemen or, come to think of it, anybody who put it all on the line for others.

Hy had been here. I could see the relief and happiness in his eyes. Now maybe he wouldn't do anything crazy.

Yeah, right . . .

I looked around. The lights were low, but my monitors flashed in a hypnotic rhythm. *Blip, blip, blip . . .* My throat felt raw from the breathing tube.

I'd sustained a lot of damage, the doctor told me. I was going to have to work hard at therapy. Well, I could do that. Given what I'd already been through, I could do anything.

I knew I shouldn't be worrying about a triviality at a time like this, but they had had to shave my head—twice. Would my hair grow back right?

Did it matter?

A nurse popped in, checked the monitors. Went away, leaving me alone.

Fuck the hair. I'm still here. Probably bald as the proverbial egg, but I'm still here!

HY RIPINSKY

The scene he walked into in Shar's office at the pier was tense in the extreme. Mick sat in Shar's desk chair, and Craig leaned against a file cabinet—positions of power. Diane D'Angelo was in one of the clients' chairs; from the way she clutched its arms, and from her tightly crossed ankles, she looked as if an invisible rope bound her there.

Craig said, "Join us, Hy. We've been having a very interesting conversation with Diane. I mean Susan. Susan Angelo, an investigator formerly of New York City, and a good friend of Jim Yatz."

"Susan was just telling us that Yatz hired her to infiltrate our offices," Mick added. "Seems he was concerned about an investigation Shar conducted for Amanda Teller last year. And there were problems at city hall that he wanted to put a good spin on by coming up clean in an additional investigation by us."

Hy looked at the woman he'd known as Diane D'Angelo. She kept her eyes down.

He said, "I've read that file. Background checks on the Pro Terra Party, its chairman, Lee Summers, and State Representative Paul Janssen. Nothing incriminating, as far as I could tell."

"But Yatz didn't know that until Diane—Susan—delivered it to him. She deleted it from the agency files, but kept a copy in her own blocked files."

Hy said, "Diane, Susan, whatever—why did you stay on here

after you turned over the information on the Teller investigation to Yatz?"

Silence. Then, "Jim told me there was a potential scandal brewing at city hall, and that he might need me here. Besides, the pay and benefits were better than what I was getting in New York."

"How the hell did you get around the agency's background checks?"

No reply.

Mick said, "Shar hired her provisionally, because Thelia was totally swamped at the time, and Jim Yatz had highly recommended her. She asked Derek for a check, but the request never got to him. Someone"—he glared at Susan Angelo—"intercepted it, and wrote Shar an excellent report."

Hy thought about that; his wife pretty much accepted her operatives' reports at face value because she knew and trusted them. Angelo must've accessed some of Derek's other background checks and copied his style.

He raised an eyebrow at Craig. "This city hall investigation—you put her on it?"

"Right. And she turned up nothing. Couldn't've, because Yatz set up a smoke screen involving disappearing files and memos. But in reality, there was only one memo that went away—from Amanda Teller to the mayor."

"Saying what?"

"Sit down, Ripinsky, and I'll tell you what the boys and girls at city hall have been up to."

MICK SAVAGE

H e and Craig and Hy debated what to do about Susan Angelo. She was being cooperative—obviously all her loyalty to her friend Yatz had evaporated upon her being found out—but her cooperation would only last so long. There wasn't anything they could have her arrested for except presenting false credentials, and even a bad public defender could get her out on bail in hours on such a charge. Then, to save her ass, she'd either take off or, more likely, sell her story to the press. And all hell would break loose.

People involved in the scandal would start lawyering up. The mayor would take a heavy hit. And they still didn't have all the answers.

Such as: Who shot Shar? Who killed Harvey Davis? Who killed Teller and Janssen?

"Shit, I don't know," Hy said. They were in the conference room, while Julia, who had returned from dropping something off at Richman Labs, was pretending to make nice to Angelo in Shar's office. "We can't keep her here against her will."

Mick said, "I don't trust her. She walks out of here, and she'll go straight to the media. D'you know how much money a story like this would bring?"

"Yeah." Craig was silent for a moment. "There may be a way to hold her." He took out his phone, speed-dialed a number.

"Tyler, it's Craig Morland. I need a favor. We've got an operative here who needs to be in protective custody . . . Witness against a number of high-level city officials . . . I know it's not a federal case, but I can't ask for help from the SFPD—some of them may be involved . . . Yes, our agency will pay you . . . A day or two, no more . . . Thanks, Tyler. I'll look for you within the hour."

He replaced the receiver. "Tyler's with the local field office, but he moonlights. He's also a good actor; he'll make Susan feel like a celebrity witness."

"Which she is, in a way," Mick said.

JULIA RAFAEL

Diane D'Angelo—Susan Angelo—smiled at her and said, "I suppose they told you about my charade."

"Yes, they did."

"That's all it was—an acting job to please my boyfriend."

"That did harm to my boss and this agency."

"How? What does it matter who's fucking who at city hall?"

"It matters that Sharon McCone is in a locked-in state and may remain there forever. It matters that Amanda Teller and Paul Janssen are dead."

D'Angelo—Angelo, whatever—sat on the edge of Shar's desk, rolling a cut-glass paperweight between her hands.

"Teller and Janssen were corrupt; they deserved what they got. McCone—she was in the way."

Julia tensed. Craig and Mick had urged her not to confront the woman, but . . .

Diane—Susan—frowned. "Jim isn't going to like me getting caught out. Or admitting to the scam." She looked down at the paperweight in her hands. "I need to tell him what happened, that they forced me to talk."

Julia didn't see what was coming until the woman rose from the desk and raised the crystal globe. She tried to shield her head—

She woke up slowly, her vision swimming, then focusing on carpet.

What carpet? Had she passed out? No way. She'd quit the drugs and booze years ago.

Footsteps coming toward her. "Jules? What happened?" Gentle

hands on her shoulders. "Jesus, there's a bloody welt on the side of your head!"

She stiffened. Then: nothing to fear. It was Craig Morland's voice; he wouldn't hurt her. But somebody had.

Oh, yeah, that *puta*, Susan Angelo. Slammed her on the head with the heavy crystal paperweight from Shar's desk.

Craig asked, "Can you sit up?"

"I don't know."

"How about turning over on your back? Or should I call nine-one-one?"

"Help me. Then we'll see."

When she was on her back again her vision swam, then focused on Craig, who was kneeling next to her.

He asked, "Did Susan do this to you?"

"Uh-huh. One minute we're talking, the next she's coming at me with Shar's paperweight."

"I think I should call for the paramedics. You could have a concussion."

"Don't. I can—" She tried to pull herself up, sank back weakly. "Maybe you better." Then she remembered about the city's emergency services' dangerously slow response times. "*Mierda*. I'll be laying around here till the middle of next week."

Craig was dialing, giving the address of the pier.

"Craig? Call my sister and let her know what happened. But ask her not to tell Tonio."

"Will do."

"And there's something I dropped off at Richman Labs. They promised it for tomorrow morning."

"I'll pick it up, don't worry."

"Thank you."

Dios, her head hurt and she felt like she was going to hurl. If she hurt this way, how bad Shar must've felt when she got shot!

RAE KELLEHER

Laura Logan didn't look any more like a porn filmmaker than the guy at Hot Shots had. She was petite, with dark shoulder-length hair, and beautifully dressed in black trousers and a flame-colored jacket. She lounged carelessly in her chair in the bar of the exclusive Barbary Hotel on Nob Hill—a place Rae had suggested they meet, thinking it might make the woman uncomfortable and put her at a disadvantage. Well, that idea hadn't worked.

Logan sipped at an expensive zinfandel she'd ordered, then said, "You're probably going to ask me how a woman could go into my industry. Exploiting other women, issues like that."

"It interests me, yes. But right now I'm even more interested in specific projects of yours—DVDs you directed for Lee Summers and the Pro Terra Party."

Logan recrossed her legs, took a long slow sip of wine. "I don't reveal information about my projects or employers."

"Under subpoena you'd have to."

"What does that mean?"

"One of the women in a lesbian film you shot was Lee Summers's daughter. A few weeks later she was found slashed to death in a SoMa alley. My attorney took a deposition from a witness this morning that indicates Summers may have killed his own daughter. I'll be talking with the DA, and I'm fairly certain the DA will want to talk with you. Eventually, you'll be called before the grand jury."

". . . Which woman was Summers's daughter?"

"The blonde."

"The one that was so out of it she didn't really know what was happening. The other was a pro; I've used her before. Jesus, Summers hired me to film his *daughter*?"

"Right. Apparently it wasn't the first time she was a featured player."

"I can't testify about this to anyone. It would kill me in the industry. I have a nice life, a little girl to support—"

"A little girl who someday may be degraded and exploited and end up with her throat cut in some dark alley just like Alicia Summers."

Logan's hand shook, sloshing wine on the table. "No! I've provided well for her, a college fund—"

"Alicia Summers was a bright, happy young woman with everything in the world to look forward to. She'd been accepted at UCLA. Then her father pimped her for party donations and influence. It only takes one evil person to destroy a life. How would you feel if your little girl encountered a Lee Summers?"

Logan gulped what was left of her wine and stared at the splatter patterns on the table for a long time. "Okay," she finally said, "I'll give a deposition to your lawyer tomorrow."

JULIA RAFAEL

"What day is it?"

"Tuesday."

"How many fingers am I holding up?"

"Two."

"Where are we?"

"Pier Twenty-four and a Half."

"What happened to you?"

"This damn fuckin' *puta* hit me on the head with a paperweight."

The paramedic's face disappeared, and Julia looked up at the fluorescent lights on the ceiling. The glare hurt her eyes, so she squeezed them shut.

"She seems okay," the medic said, "but she should be hospitalized overnight. Head trauma can be tricky."

"Right." Craig.

Julia said, "I want to go home."

"Follow the doctor's orders."

"He's not a doctor."

"He knows a hell of a lot more than you do."

She sighed, gave in. Wasn't worth fighting when she was so tired.

In the ambulance she asked the attendant, "Where're you taking me?"

"SF General."

Well, at least she'd be close to Shar.

MICK SAVAGE

He wedged the Harley into a spot between two sports cars on Filbert Street in the upscale Cow Hollow neighborhood. The address Susan Angelo had listed on her application for employment was a two-story sugar cube of a building mid-block. A light shone in a small entry with two mailboxes and intercoms on its wall. He approached quietly and looked at the names on the boxes.

No Angelo or D'Angelo.

He rang the bell of the first-floor unit, but got no response. A woman's voice replied on the intercom of the top unit; it wasn't Susan's. He asked for Diane D'Angelo, and the woman said she wasn't there.

"But this is her place?"

"No. She gets mail sometimes, but she doesn't live here."

"May I come up and talk with you?"

"Why?"

"I'm a private investigator with the agency where Diane works. She may be in trouble."

Silence.

"Look, I've got identification. I can slip it under your door—"

"No, I'll come down."

He waited. The fog was sailing overhead, bypassing this exclusive enclave on its way to obscure the less privileged neighborhoods. It was chilly; San Francisco summer wouldn't arrive till

September. He thought of Shar: how she loved the warm, golden autumn days. . . .

And again she'd get to enjoy them. His relief on hearing she was going to be okay had made him weak; the tension he'd been carrying around since the night of her attack had flowed out of him. He hadn't thought it possible, after what he'd witnessed that last night at the Brandt Institute, that his aunt would live, let alone be whole again. But by some miracle she would.

The building's door opened, and a heavyset woman with short gray hair looked out. "Okay, where's this identification?" she asked.

He took out both his private investigator's and driver's licenses and passed them to her. The door closed, then opened a few moments later. "All right," she said, "we can talk here in the lobby. My neighbors are only a few yards away. You try anything, they'll be on you pretty quick."

Mick stepped onto what she called the lobby. It was small with a mirrored wall and no furnishings. The woman took up most of the space.

"Thank you, Ms. . . . ?"

"Kelly. Mimi Kelly."

"I appreciate you talking with me. How do you know Diane?"

"I don't."

"But she gets mail here."

"You ever heard of a drop?"

"So d'you hold the mail or forward it?"

"Forward to a P.O. box."

"What about phone calls?"

"I screen them, relay them to another machine."

"Will you give me the phone and P.O. box numbers?"

She shifted her stance, folded her arms across her pendulous breasts. "I don't give out that information; this is a business for me."

"You have other clients, then."

"Honey, I got clients whose names would make your eyes bug out. People want a fancy address for one reason or another. And I'm happy to live at that address."

"You have backing for your business? Somebody who finances your living expenses?"

"Once, a long time ago, I did. My uncle, he's dead. Left me all his money; now I own the building."

Mick's guess was that Susan Angelo had fled the city or had gone to ground at the place where she really lived. He thought about what she'd admitted to them, then took out his phone and checked San Francisco listings. None, but the one he was looking for could be easily accessed via search engine. He got it and moments later he was headed downhill to the Marina district.

Quiet in the entry courtyard of this Spanish-style house on Mallorca Way—a building of a type predominant in this bayside neighborhood. Sweet smell of some night-blooming plant and pungent odor of recently watered earth. In spite of the drifting fog he thought of summer nights at his grandparents' house in San Diego, where his father had parked the family while he went out on the road with other people's bands before he made it on his own. His uncle John—who was currently hanging around Shar and Hy's place and annoying the hell out of Hy—lived with his new wife and two boys in the old homeplace now. Maybe after Shar was better, they'd pay a visit. . . .

He went to the front door of the house, hit the bell. Chimes rang inside, but no one came. There were lights on in the room to the right of the door. He rang again. No response.

Well, maybe his theory had been wrong.

He was about to turn away when he noticed a faint odor that contrasted sharply with that of the plants in the courtyard. He sniffed. Cordite. A gun had been fired here recently, maybe more than once.

He put his hand on the door latch. It moved. He hesitated.

He wasn't armed, wasn't even firearms-qualified. In fact, he had never so much as held a gun in his hands. And he sure as hell didn't want to walk into another scene like the one at the lodge in Big Sur. That experience had convinced him he couldn't take blood and gore.

Besides, entering struck him as an unnecessary risk. A shooter could be waiting inside and blast him when he walked in. Or he could jeopardize a possible crime scene—and his license—by inadvertently tampering with evidence.

But maybe somebody in there needed help? If so, he couldn't do anything for them. Only the paramedics could.

Maybe he was rationalizing, but there was no way he wanted to step through that door.

He took out his phone and dialed 911. Then, since Craig and Adah lived only a couple of blocks away, he called them and asked for their supportive presence.

CRAIG MORLAND

Come on, Dom—you know me. Give me a break here."

Craig watched Adah as she faced down Dominick Rayborn, the investigator who had replaced her on the SFPD's homicide squad. Around them squad cars' lights pulsed and an ambulance pulled away. Two body bags had been removed from Jim Yatz's house. A press van from the local CBS affiliate had just driven up and double-parked next to others from ABC and NBC.

Rayborn saw it, and his sharp-featured face ticked with annoyance. "Dammit, Adah, I can't stand here jawing with you. Not when some asshole with a microphone is about to light on me."

"You've cleared and secured the scene. You'll need to interview our operative who called this in. We can all go down to the Hall—"

"No, that's the last thing I need—" He broke off, said to a uniform, "Get her out of here!" Her being a TV newswoman who had slipped past the police barricade. "The goddamn media vultures'll be waiting on the steps of the Hall."

"So come to my place."

He hesitated. "Irregular, but it might work. You'll have this operative there—what's his name?—Mick Savage."

"Yes. Craig and I are only a couple of blocks away; when Mick called, we walked over. He can walk back with us, to avoid attracting attention. Then you shake the press vans and come by."

He shook his head. "I'll go with you. They'll never expect me to leave on foot."

Craig loved the apartment. It had been Adah's for years before he met her. Spacious and airy, with white walls and great splashes of colorful furnishings and artwork, and a large deck that they shared with the neighboring unit. The neighbors were an older couple in their late sixties; they were gardeners and often shared the vegetables from their small patch with Adah and him. A few weeks ago, the four of them had gone in together on a gas grill from Costco.

Now home seemed strange, with the rambunctious new cats—still called That One and The Other—locked in the bedroom and the somber-faced, sharp-featured homicide detective perched on the edge of their red sofa. He'd declined a soft drink or coffee, taped Mick's story about how he'd come to be at Yatz's house, then gone silent, his fingers laced together, staring at the floor.

"Our turn, Dom," Adah prompted.

He looked up, distracted from his thoughts. "Okay," he said. "The vics are Jim Yatz and a woman with two sets of ID on her—Diane D'Angelo and Susan Angelo. One of your operatives, as Mr. Savage has told me. Our preliminary findings indicate a murder-suicide; Yatz blew her away, then turned his thirty-eight on himself. Neighbors to the right of the house heard an argument going on and turned up their TV to cover the noise. This was about nine o'clock; fifteen minutes later, when the husband got up to get something from the kitchen, everything was quiet."

Craig said, "Don't you find it peculiar that two other people involved in city or state government were recently killed in an apparent murder-suicide?"

"You mean Teller and Janssen. The sheriff's department down in Monterey County has been in close touch with us; they've classified it a homicide. In this case it's different: no injections, and obvious powder burns on Yatz's hands, apparently from his own gun. There's also evidence that Angelo had been living there for a fair amount of time."

Mick said, "So Angelo went home, told Yatz we had evidence on him on DVD, that she'd admitted to everything, and we were taking it to the DA. He shot her, then killed himself."

"Everything points to that. We'll know more when we get reports from ballistics and the ME's office."

Adah said, "I'd like to see copies of those reports."

Rayborn nodded. "We can work together on this. I'll appreciate any input you can offer, and I'll reciprocate." His solemn face softened. "I know your record, Adah. You were one of the best, and I'm glad to see you haven't burned out. This job . . ." He shrugged. "Maybe I'll be applying to McCone Investigations myself in a few years."

If there still was a McCone Investigations, Craig thought. Shar wasn't out of the woods by a long shot, and he didn't think the rest of them had the heart to carry on without her.

WEDNESDAY, JULY 23

HY RIPINSKY

He filled his coffee mug, then went to the sitting room to watch the morning news. The story of the Yatz and Angelo murder-suicide had made the national reports, bringing with it a rehash of the Teller-Janssen case. The media, of course, were eager to link the two, in spite of denials by officials in both jurisdictions. There was also mention of Angelo's "double life" as an operative of the McCone agency, whose owner, Sharon McCone, had recently been shot by an intruder at the firm's offices. Details of her present condition were "unavailable."

Hy watched for a few moments, then pressed the off button on the remote. Craig had called him around two in the morning to tell him what had gone down at the Yatz house, so none of this was new to him, but he'd been interested in what kind of treatment the press was giving the story. At least no one had ferreted out that Shar had been at the Brandt Institute or brought back to SF General. The story of her shooting had dropped off the radar after a few days, when inquiries to the agency and other people who knew her failed to bring results. Now, he supposed, he and the others would have to field annoying phone calls and encounters again.

The door to the guest room opened and seconds later John appeared, wrapped in one of Hy's old bathrobes—a blackwatch plaid that he'd never particularly liked. John's blond hair stood up in spikes and he yawned and blinked groggily at Hy.

"Shar?" he asked. "Any change?"

"I spoke with the nurse a while ago. She's resting comfortably."

"What the hell does that mean?"

"She's no longer in crisis, she's aware of her surroundings—"

"In short, just like she was before she crashed." John sank heavily into the armchair.

"Not exactly. The bullet and bone fragments have been removed, the clot is gone—"

"And she's irreparably damaged."

John's pessimism was getting to Hy. He picked up his coffee mug and took it into the kitchen. Ralph, their orange tabby, looked up at him from his food bowl, then went on eating.

Hy had spent most of the previous evening sitting beside his wife and watching her face as she lay in the silent motionless state he'd gotten used to. She was no longer in intensive care, but on another floor, in a step-down unit where the nurses came around frequently to monitor her; they slipped in and out, smiling reassuringly at him, checking Shar's vitals, making notes on her chart. Once in a while he thought he saw her eyelids flutter and imagined a facial tic. But mostly she lay still and waxen.

Gathering strength to get well. Strength for the long fight ahead.

He checked his watch, saw it was time he went to the pier for the staff meeting Adah had called for this morning. That would occupy the time until he was due to see Shar's attending physician at one o'clock.

RAE KELLEHER

She came into the conference room ten minutes late, slipped into a chair next to Mick. He was taking notes—long, erratic scratches with arrows connecting them—and Craig was speaking.

"... So here's the theory we're going to present to the DA's office: Amanda Teller heard rumors that someone was making sex videos of city officials. She came to the agency and asked Shar for deep background on the Pro Terra Party, in particular Lee Summers and Paul Janssen. She wrote a memo to the mayor, probably detailing what she'd found out, but Jim Yatz intercepted it."

Sex videos?

"Was there actually a memo?" Derek Ford asked. "Or was that more of Yatz's attempt to muddy the facts?"

"Don't know," Craig said. "What I do know is that Teller's long-term aide, Harvey Davis, had become disenchanted with her. Davis started leaking vague information to me after Yatz hired us to look into purportedly missing documents at city hall. Frankly, I thought Davis was behaving theatrically, had a Deep Throat fixation. He gave me a key to his condo in case something happened to him, and after he was shot I went there and found the videos. He also told me about Teller and Janssen's plans to meet at Big Sur; the surveillance tapes that I made of their conversation at the Spindrift Lodge suggest that Janssen was on very shaky emotional territory, and that Teller took advantage of it to make him sign some kind of document pertaining to the videos."

Rae thought, *We've been working on the same case!*

She started to speak, but Mick said, "We assume the videos were made for the purposes of Janssen and the Pro Terra Party, but we don't know who made them or who—"

"I do."

All eyes fixed on Rae as she told them about Lee Summers, his daughter, Callie O'Leary, Hot Shots, and Laura Logan—who was giving a deposition to her lawyer as they spoke. Then everybody began talking at once.

Over the din, Adah said, "Okay, hold it! I want Rae, Craig, and Mick to share their notes and start putting a timeline together. Patrick, you create one of your flowcharts. Everybody else pitch in. This is big—way too big to delay on. And Hy, can you alert Glenn Solomon to what's going on? We need a heavy-hitting attorney to bring this to the DA."

"What about who shot Shar?" Rae said somewhat plaintively. "We're losing sight of that."

"Not for a moment we aren't. It's all going to come out now."

JULIA RAFAEL

Breakfast in the hospital: runny eggs, some kind of sausage she couldn't identify, dry toast, weak coffee. She left most of it. Then the doc said she was okay, the X-rays had been negative, no concussion, and she could go. She got dressed and asked the nurse for Shar's room number. But when she finally found the nurses' station on that floor, they wouldn't let Julia see her. Limited visitors, they said.

Disappointed, she went out into the watery sunlight—fog burning off—and stood wondering what to do next. Get some rest today, the doc had told her. Sure, she'd said. But she had things to do. She took out her phone and dialed Craig. He didn't pick up. She called the agency. Ted was terse with her, told her they had a situation brewing and to get her ass over there.

Julia broke the connection. Her nose still throbbed from when she'd run into the grape stake, she'd been bashed on the head last night, and now she was being ordered around. Well, Ted probably didn't know about the head bashing and her hospitalization; he'd left before that *almeja* had attacked her. So she'd get her ass over to the pier, but first she'd stop at Richman Labs; they'd promised her a report on the duffel bag by nine.

On the bus from the labs to the pier—where her car still sat—she read the report they'd given her. The bag had been manufactured in Taiwan; it was a brand that had been sold at quality luggage stores until it was discontinued three years ago. Smudged fingerprints on the leather outside. No markings to identify the owner. Two small patches of blood on the cloth lining—AB negative.

Rare. What was Haven Dietz's blood type? Her attacker must've gotten some on himself, and then in the bag. Was there blood on the money? She'd have to call the Peepleses and ask.

So what was this "situation" at the pier? Shar? *Dios mio!* Had Shar died?

No. Ted had sounded excited, energized. If Shar had died, he would've been crying. Besides, Julia had just been to the nurses' station on Shar's floor; they'd said she was resting, not dead.

The bus pulled into its last stop on Harrison. Julia got out and walked the few blocks to the pier.

MICK SAVAGE

The case was coming together so fast it was almost scary. He sat at the keyboard at Shar's desk—because hers was the biggest office—inputting the facts Craig read to him. On the floor, Patrick crawled over one of the big whiteboard flowcharts he used to keep track of cases in progress, adding details, wiping out others, creating a timeline. In their separate offices, the rest of the staff were fact-checking, establishing a rock-solid foundation. Hy had gone to consult with Shar's friend Glenn Solomon. Glenn would love this case: he loathed corrupt politicians.

Of course, who didn't?

Mick felt higher than he had since Shar was shot. Miles higher than he'd felt since he and Craig had walked into that grim scene at Big Sur. Then and later, riding his bike to Monterey, he'd felt hollow and afraid; at Jim Yatz's house last night he'd been more in control, able to handle the situation right. And now—this made the other things worth it. This was the conclusion of the hunt.

And maybe the answer to who had attacked Shar.

Thelia came into the room, handed a sheaf of papers to Craig, and went away. Craig read them, handed them to Mick, and pointed out a couple of lines: on the day before he was killed, Paul Janssen had ordered his broker at Edward Jones to sell off a number of stocks from his considerable portfolio; they had yielded more than five hundred thousand dollars, and the funds had gone into his cash account, upon which Janssen could have written a check on Monday.

Paying Teller off, in addition to signing whatever document she'd brought him.

Mick glanced at Craig. Craig nodded and went to give the information to Patrick. Mick entered it into the computer.

Derek relayed more deep background on Teller. She'd been linked romantically with Janssen for a short time before his successful run for the state house of representatives. It was not common knowledge, but the source—a blogger with excellent contacts in state government—was reliable.

More information into the timeline.

Patrick said, "This is shaping up really well. Can somebody get me another whiteboard?"

Mick hit the intercom for Ted, and shortly afterward Ted's assistant Kendra hurried in with one.

Julia was out, interviewing a domestic employee of Amanda Teller whose name had surfaced earlier. Rae was in Lafayette, talking again with Senta Summers. She'd attempted to contact Cheryl Fitzgerald, the remaining cofounder of the Pro Terra Party who had threatened Summers the night before, but her office said she had left unexpectedly for Italy. Fled with a fistful of blackmail money, Rae claimed. She'd ask Hy to put one of the people in RI's Rome office onto locating Fitzgerald. Adah had hired an operative from another agency to keep tabs on Lee Summers; he was at party headquarters, where he often stayed for days on end.

Hy returned. Glenn Solomon was in full battle mode, he said. Ready to roll. How soon could they have the timeline and files ready?

Soon, Mick told him. Very soon.

But as he went back to his keyboard, he found himself thinking that even though everything fit something was wrong. There was a missing piece. Who had gone to the pier that night and put the bullet in Shar's head?

SHARON McCONE

*L*ooking at the ceiling again. God, I hate ceilings! I want to sit up. *Get up. Walk out of here into the sunshine. Breathe fresh air. They've taken me off the ventilator again; I could do it, if I could just make my damn limbs work right.*

My fingers tried to make a fist—

They moved!

Just a fraction of an inch, but they moved!

A wild elation coursed through me. I tried to call out for the nurse.

"*Ack.*"

My throat was raw, the sound weak and pathetic.

But I'd made a sound!

"*Ack . . . ack . . . ack . . .*"

I sounded like an asthmatic duck, but so what?

I moved my right index finger—tremulous, tiny motion, but all my own!

"*Ack . . . ack . . . ack . . .*"

I'd get their attention yet.

The doctor, what was it he'd said? The remaining crap was out of my head—well, he'd spoken more eloquently and technically than that, but what it boiled down to was that the crap was gone, there was no more swelling, and I should start regaining bodily functions.

"*Ack!*"

A nurse appeared around the curtains. She moved forward swiftly, took my pulse, looked into my eyes.

"*Ack!*"

She nodded. "I'll page Dr. Travers, Ms. McCone. I think he'll be as happy as you seem to be right now."

CRAIG MORLAND

He, Hy, and Glenn Solomon left the DA's office in the Hall of Justice at Sixth and Bryant Streets and rode the elevator down.

"It's not an airtight case yet," Glenn said, "but it's good."

Craig said, "It still doesn't link the Pro Terra people with what happened to McCone."

Hy turned to him. "'What happened'? Don't sugarcoat it: my wife was *shot*!"

Tempers were flaring. Craig knew it all too well; at the Bureau, when a case was coming together, agents—male and female—were often on the verge of physically thrashing it out.

"Sorry," he said. "I spoke carelessly."

A pause. Then Hy said, "That's okay. Since Shar crashed I've been flying on empty. I'm heading to the hospital now. When I see her I'll feel better."

He turned, cut across the street to the lot where he'd parked. Craig watched him go, then sighed and turned back to Solomon.

The big, silver-haired attorney was attired as usual in an expensive tailor-made suit. He and his wife, society interior decorator Bette Silver, were good friends of Shar's and had been visibly shaken when Craig had run into them at the Brandt Institute last week. Glenn was known as a fierce litigator who could demolish an adversary's case with a single caustic remark, but once he left the legal arena, he became his true self: an entertaining companion, a kind and compassionate friend, and a strong advocate for those in need. Or as Bette had once put it, "A pussycat who roars for a living."

Solomon tapped him on the shoulder. "When was the last time you ate?"

Craig shrugged. "Yesterday. I forget."

"Come with me."

They got into Glenn's Jaguar and drove over to Franklin Street near City Hall, where Glenn handed the car over to a valet parker at a small café called Bistro Americaine. Glenn was known there— he was probably known in most good restaurants in the city—and they were quickly seated in a booth. When Craig looked at the menu his stomach lurched, so Glenn ordered for him: steak, fries, a side of creamed spinach. Bottle of a chewy zinfandel for the two of them.

"Heart-stopper meal," Glenn said, "but the wine'll cut the grease."

Craig smiled weakly.

"Actually I wanted to talk privately with you," Glenn added.

"About what?"

"The issue of what happened to Sharon. In the brief time I had to review it, the information you presented to me—and I presented to the DA—didn't indicate any link to her shooting."

The feeling of dread that he'd been entertaining all day intensified. "That was my take on it."

"I don't mean to say these people aren't killers; Lee Summers is my candidate for the murders of his daughter, Harvey Davis, and Teller and Janssen. But they didn't do Yatz and Angelo—I've spoken to the SFPD and ME's office, and they believe that was just what it appeared to be, a murder-suicide. And my gut tells me none of them did Shar."

Craig rubbed his eyes. The waiter came with the wine, and he waited till the whole ritual of smelling the cork and tasting a sip was done before he asked, "Is that just a gut-level reaction, or is there some basis for it in fact?"

"There's a basis. There was no need for them or anyone connected with them to enter the pier and search files. They had access to everything they needed to know."

Craig sat up straighter. "How?"

"When I came to pick you up at the pier this afternoon, I took a close look at D'Angelo's e-mails, then I asked Derek to take an even closer look. She sent copies of everything to Lee Summers."

"Playing both sides, was she?"

"Three sides, I'd say. She was working for McCone Investigations, living with Jim Yatz, and selling out both to Summers."

"So where does that leave us?"

"Square one, my friend. Square one."

HY RIPINSKY

He'd received a message on his voice mail, having had to turn the phone off for the conference in the DA's office. Halfway to the parking lot he played it.

Ben Travers: "I have good news about your wife. Call me as soon as you can."

He tried calling Travers back, couldn't reach him. Ran into the lot, reclaimed his Mustang, and sped across town, weaving in and out among slow drivers. At SF General he parked in a physician's space and rushed inside.

Shar's floor was quiet; no one was at the nurses' station for the moment. He went down the hall to his wife's room, pushed aside the curtains around her bed.

A nurse was sponging off Shar's face; it looked small and pale beneath the bandages that covered her head. The nurse turned and smiled at him.

"Mr. Ripinsky, we've been waiting for you. Haven't we, Ms. McCone?"

Shar said, "*Ack!*"

He stared at her.

"*Ack!*"

It was the most beautiful sound she'd ever uttered.

JULIA RAFAEL

She slumped in her chair, staring at the duffel bag on her desk. She'd spent the afternoon phoning local luggage stores—over fifty in all. Most hadn't carried this particular brand; the others didn't keep sales records going back three years. Dead end, unless she wanted to extend her search to other communities, and she didn't have the energy for that right now.

The phone buzzed, and she picked up. Ted said, "A Lt. Morrison on line two."

She'd called Dave Morrison, the head of the team working Haven Dietz's murder, to ask him to find out Dietz's blood type.

"Type O positive," he told her.

Earlier he'd asked her why she needed the information. She'd said something vague about a lead, and then he'd had to take another call. Now he repeated the request.

She badly wanted to tell him about the money and the duffel bag. Dump the case in his lap and move on. But if she did, she'd violate the bond of confidentiality with the Peepleses by admitting they—and she and the agency—had covered up evidence. But evidence of what? It wasn't Dietz's blood in the duffel, and she really couldn't prove it was linked to the attack or murder.

"I thought I had a lead, but it turns out I don't," she said.

"Why don't you tell me about this lead?"

Julia began the tale she'd thought up while being put on hold by the luggage store. "An informant spun this wild story about finding bloodstained clothing near Dietz's apartment building. He said he'd had it tested, and the blood was type AB negative. But he couldn't tell me what lab he'd had it tested at, and—after I called you—it turned out that he couldn't produce the clothes. Then he admitted they'd never existed."

Dios, Shar had told her this job would turn her into a liar. Now she'd gone world-class.

Morrison sighed. "Informants . . . They can be a pain in the ass. Hope this one didn't take you for much."

"Nah, he was in it for the publicity."

After she hung up the receiver, she slumped back again, brooding over the duffel bag.

There were footsteps on the catwalk, and Rae came into the office. "God, I'm exhausted!" she exclaimed and flopped on her back on the floor.

"Where've you been?"

"Lafayette, interviewing Senta Summers again. No surprises there. It's hotter than hell in the East Bay, and traffic got snarled near the Caldecott Tunnel."

"I've never been there—I mean, past the tunnel."

"Pretty suburbs, rolling hills. But it's getting so damn overpopulated. Every place in California is getting overpopulated. What's that?"

"What's what?"

"The bag on your desk."

"A big pain in the *culo*." She briefly summarized her theory about the bag.

Rae listened, massaging her temples with her fingertips.

"Okay," she said. "Your reasoning sounds solid. Whoever attacked Dietz bled, and some of it came off on the bag's lining. If you were a cop, you could go to databases of known offenders and try for a DNA match. But you're not a cop."

"And I can't break my agreement of confidentiality with the Peeples. I was the one who told them to keep the money in their safe."

"Because there was no evidence of a crime. You're entitled to hold money you find on your property any place you choose. Even the bloodstains don't prove a crime—their son could've cut himself shaving the day he stashed the cash."

"Right. So what should I do? I've never had to deal with anything this complicated before."

Rae was silent, her knees bent, arms outflung on the carpet.

"Let Shar hear the evidence. She'll know."

"How? She's fighting for her life."

Rae sat up, blue eyes wide. "Didn't anybody tell you? She's completely conscious, making sounds, and moving a little—a miracle. Give her a few days. This case will wait till then."

Julia put her head in her hands and cried with relief.

MONDAY, JULY 28

SHARON McCONE

*T*oday is the day I really start living again.

I can move—minimally. I can talk, even if it does come out garbled most of the time. I'm responding to therapy.

But best of all, they're all coming this afternoon. We're holding a staff meeting right here in my new room at the Brandt Institute.

It was a bigger room with two upholstered chairs and an even better view of the eucalyptus grove. Same restful blue walls, but I now found myself drawn to the bright spots of color of the flowers people had sent and a poster of Rae's new book jacket that she'd tacked up.

Bright color, a symbol of action, liveliness, my future.

Hy, of course, had briefed me all along on the investigations. Indictments were being prepared against Pro Terra Party Chairman Lee Summers, his aides, and a dozen city and state officials. Summers was under investigation for the murders of his daughter, Harvey Davis, Amanda Teller, and Paul Janssen; whether he'd done them or hired them out made no difference. He was going down.

But it was doubtful he or one of his associates had put the bullet in my head.

That left the case Julia was working on, which she was going to present to me this afternoon. And if my shooting wasn't connected with that—then what?

A run-of-the-mill burglary that I interrupted? The random situation of being in the wrong place at the wrong time?

No, that didn't feel right.

One in the afternoon. I could actually turn my head a little to see the small crystal clock that Hy had bought me. The agency staff were coming at one-thirty. I felt like a kid who was having a birthday party.

A bald-as-an-egg kid.

The nurses kept reassuring me that my hair would grow back in. But when they'd removed the bandages, I'd wondered. Jesus, what vanity! But I'd always had such thick, manageable hair—probably my best feature.

No, from now on your best feature will be walking and talking. Making love with Hy. Eventually driving and flying. Living—pure sweet living.

Promptly at one-thirty they filed in—Julia, Mick, Craig, Rae, and Adah. In the interest of keeping the meeting small, we'd decided against including Patrick, Derek, and Thelia. Hy had come a few minutes earlier and leaned against the wall, making room for the others.

Adah chaired the meeting, asking first Craig, then Mick, and finally Rae to sum up the city hall investigation. The indictments had come down, the accused had lawyered up. Lee Summers was being held without bail for the murders of Teller and Janssen. The chief evidence against him was the document Teller had made Janssen sign, admitting to collaborating with Summers in choosing his victims for the sex videos: instead of destroying it, Summers had carelessly left it in a locked drawer in his office. The Pro Terra Party—which had only been a vehicle for getting into office lawmakers whose votes would financially benefit Summers and a handful of associates—had been disbanded, although some environmentalists Hy knew were thinking of reviving it in its original incarnation. There was no tangible evidence to link Summers or any of his cohorts to my shooting, but the authorities were investigating Summers's involvement in his daughter Alicia's murder.

One case closed.

"The mayor," Hy said, "is weathering the storm with his usual diplomacy. City operations go on uninterrupted."

Adah said, "Julia? Your case?"

She stood, visibly nervous. I knew why: everybody else had closed their investigations; she—a relatively new kid on the block—had hit a wall. I tried to smile reassuringly at her, but smiles were not my forte these days.

She gave a detailed synopsis of the case, holding up pictures from her file as she had the last time.

"What bothers me," she ended, "is why Larry Peeples would leave a hundred thousand dollars at his parents' place and not try to retrieve it till recently."

Think, Julia. Maybe he *didn't leave it.*

Maybe he couldn't *retrieve it.*

"And if he attacked Dietz for it, why did he nurse her back to health?" Julia went on, "The attack was savage—no simple mugging. And the perp brought along his own bag to stash the money in. I asked the parents what Larry's blood type is—O positive. It was AB negative in the duffel."

Because Peeples didn't attack her. It was the perp's blood.

"But it stands to reason he put the money under the floor in that tack room. Whoever did it had knowledge of the place, and an excuse to be there in case somebody saw them. I called Ben Gold before I came over here, asked him for yet another follow-up interview later this afternoon. And tomorrow, I'll talk with the parents again."

I moved a finger toward the file—a tiny gesture, but Hy caught it and told Julia to hold it up where I could see it. She turned the pages slowly until I found what I was looking for.

Somebody else was familiar with the property. And could've explained away his being there.

I said, "Pebbers."

"I don't—"

"Pebters!" God, this was aggravating, knowing what I wanted to say but not being able to articulate it.

Hy said, "She means pictures. She wants to see the pictures again."

Thank God somebody could understand me.

Julia turned to the pictures: formal headshot of Dietz before the attack; group shot with the staff at the financial management firm where she'd been employed; informal and badly lighted snap of her in front of her apartment. Formal shot of Peeples; Larry with his parents at the vineyard; Larry and Ben Gold with Seal Rock in the background. I studied them.

Yes!

I wanted to point to the picture, but my strength was flagging. Everybody was watching me, but I could only twitch a finger. I glanced at Hy; he nodded, encouraging me.

I said, "Bole."

Dammit!

They waited. I looked around, then focused on Mick. He was wearing a silver bracelet that he'd bought on vacation in Santa Fe a couple of years ago. Intricate handcrafted links, like the ones my hand had grazed when the flash from my assailant's gun briefly illuminated them. Like the metal links in my hallucinations when I'd crashed. Like the bracelet the man in the photograph wore.

I stared fixedly at Mick's bracelet. No one spoke; I supposed they all thought I'd lost it. Mick shifted his stance, I shifted my stare. He glanced around and frowned. I kept staring.

He said, "Shar? What's wrong?"

I didn't take my gaze off the bracelet. He looked down, frowned again.

It was Julia who got it. She glanced from Mick's wrist to the photos she'd shown me. Looked into my eyes.

I blinked once.

"Ben Gold," she said. "Dietz told Peeples about the embezzlement, and he told Gold."

I blinked once again.

There was a stir in the room, a collective hiss of anger and sigh of relief. Then everybody started talking.

"Gold ripped off Haven Dietz, then hid the money at the Peeples' place."

"He waited till he was sure nobody suspected him before he asked Larry to go away with him."

"Larry refused—he was moving back to Sonoma to learn the wine business."

"Did Gold kill him?"

"What did he do with his body?"

"Gold's kept in touch with the family, plans to go back and get the money someday. He thinks it's still in the tack room."

"So who was it that was skulking around the night Julia spent there?"

"Haven Dietz, of course. She overheard my conversation with Judy Peeples. I should've figured that out sooner."

"When Gold found out the parents hired us to investigate, he broke into the pier, looking for our case files."

"Why'd he take a gun along?"

"Maybe he knew about the guard. Or maybe he just felt safer armed."

They'd summed up what I was thinking: it wasn't personal. I'd just gotten in the way.

I looked for Hy, but he was gone.

Now the craziness starts. . . .

HY RIPINSKY

He stopped at the RI offices to pick up a weapon, some handcuffs, and a voice-activated tape recorder. He had carry permits and kept .45s in locked bedside tables in all three of Shar's and his homes, but he didn't like to keep one on his person or even in his car. Too much chance of theft, too much chance of having it turned against him.

The previous year, after the offices of the company then called RKI had been bombed, he'd relocated the business to a very different type of building from the converted warehouse on Green Street: a newish high-rise on Second Street near the Transbay Terminal. Building security was top-notch, RI's additional security on its three floors even better. It would take a lot more than a homemade explosive device to bring the firm down again.

In his office—spartan, functional, the only luxury item being a leather sofa that was comfortable on long nights when a situation was brewing—he paused by the phone, considering a call to Len Weathers for assistance. No, he'd already decided Weathers was out of his life for good. Instead he called home and spoke to Brother John.

John was waiting on the sidewalk in front of the house when Hy pulled up in his Mustang. "Okay, let's get this thing done," he said as he got in.

It was nearly five o'clock; the evening fog had blown in early and brought with it a winter-like dusk. Hy switched on his lights.

"So where is this bastard?" John asked.

"I called the store where he works; he's probably home by now. Loft in SoMa. We can be there in fifteen minutes."

"And then?"

"I've got my plans for him."

John visibly shrank from the hardness in his voice. Hy realized his brother-in-law had never seen him in this mode; few people in his present life had, except for Shar.

He said, "Don't worry—there won't be any killing."

"Good."

This from the guy who'd been itching for blood from day one. Well, he was glad to know John wasn't a killer. He wasn't any more either.

The building where Ben Gold had his loft was a former factory on Clarence Street—a short block near the Giants' ballpark. New windows in a century-old facade; faded lettering on the brick— Shea's Iron Works. Outer foyer with surveillance cameras and intercoms. No answer at Gold's.

Hy began pushing buzzers. Most residents didn't answer. One who—from the numbering system—appeared to be on Gold's floor, did. Hy said that he was Gold's attorney and needed to see him on urgent business. The disembodied voice—male, female?— said Ben was on vacation, had gone to the Sonoma Valley to stay with friends for a few days.

Hy turned away, said to John, "Julia mentioned she'd called Gold for another follow-up interview today. It must've spooked him. I'll bet he's gone to the Peepleses' winery for the money. He told Julia he was moving to LA soon to pursue his film career; he's moved the departure date up."

They went back to the car without speaking, and Hy drove to the nearby Bay Bridge on-ramp.

Bright lights outside a large house at the top of a rise; dark driveway that meandered among vineyards. Hy pulled the Mustang onto the shoulder close to a low stone fence and cut the lights and engine.

Beside him, John was taking deep measured breaths—calming himself.

"Easy approach on foot," Hy told his brother-in-law.

"Lots of light up there, though. I can see the individual branches of those oak trees."

"Lights're trained up on the trees and house. I don't see any in the windows."

Hy reached around John and took from the glove box the .45, the set of handcuffs, and the tape recorder he'd brought from the office.

John said, "You bring some of those for me, too?"

"No. One pair of cuffs and one recorder is enough, and I don't hand over firearms to people who aren't licensed to use them."

"Funny, for somebody who used to be such a loose cannon." Hy could hear a measure of relief in John's voice; he'd probably never held a gun, much less fired one.

"*Used* to be?"

"Well, yeah. I guess we wouldn't be here if the old fires were completely banked."

"Damn right."

Hy got out of the car, and John followed. John was wearing a light-colored shirt; Hy tossed him the black microfiber jacket he wore over his dark T-shirt. John's blond hair was bright, even on a moonless night. "Pull up that hood," Hy told him.

They started up the driveway, keeping to the side next to the stone wall. The vineyards were quiet except for the occasional light breeze that rustled the leaves of the grape plants. The air was warm, its smell earthy. The house loomed before them, silhouetted against the dark sky. At first Hy thought he'd been right about there being no lights in its windows, but then he glimpsed slanting yellow shafts coming from the rear to the left.

When they reached the top of the drive, he motioned for John to follow him under the oak trees. Led him around the spots that shone upward on their gnarled branches. Stopped and held up his hand. Pointed at himself and then at the back of the house.

Stay here. I'll check it out.

John nodded.

In a crouch Hy moved through the oaks to the house. Sidled along the wall. Outside the first shaft of light, he stopped. The window was open, and he heard voices.

"... Great dinner, Mrs. Peeples. I really appreciate you letting me stay the night. I so enjoyed the times I spent here with Larry." A youngish male.

Murmured reply in an older woman's voice.

"And I'm so sorry Mr. Peeples is away at that conference."

"He'll be sorry he missed you."

"If it's okay, I'd like to take a walk before turning in. It's so warm here—unlike in the city—and everything's so fragrant."

Another murmured reply.

Hy slipped back along the side of the house, clicked his fingers at John, motioning him to follow.

They were halfway to the rear windows when the lights went out. Another flashed at the back of the house. A door opened and closed. Footsteps swished—moving over grass—then crunched on gravel.

Hy kept going, John close behind.

They reached the back of the house, and Hy touched John's shoulder, signaling for him to stop. Ahead of them a figure was disappearing into yet another oak grove. Hy measured the open space they'd have to cross, waited till the figure disappeared, then gestured for John to follow him in a crouch.

At the other side of the grove he saw a stable—big place, not like the one that he and Shar housed their horses in at their ranch. The tack room would be there.

He signaled to John and they moved forward. Through the open front doors, where the familiar smells of hay and manure greeted him. Past the stalls, where the horses—five or six, he couldn't tell in the dim light—pawed and snorted at the intrusion. There was a faint glow in the doorway to the tack room. He motioned for John to stop, then eased close to the doorjamb.

A man knelt inside, flashlight trained on the floor, feeling around at the boards.

Hy restrained himself. Waited to see if the bastard pried up the right one.

The man lifted the board, shone the light down. Gasped and dropped the wood.

Hy raised the .45 in both hands. "Stand up, Gold, and stay still."

Ben Gold panicked instead. Dropped the flashlight into the space where the duffel bag had been and rushed forward. Hy almost shot him. His momentary hesitation gave Gold time to dodge past him.

But the kid didn't get far. Behind him Hy heard a grunt and a thud. Then another thud, louder than the first.

John exclaimed, "Ha!"

Hy retrieved the still-glowing flashlight and shone it around. John was standing with one foot on the small of Gold's back. Gold wriggled feebly against the weight, then lay still.

Hy said, "Don't crush him, for God's sake."

"Why not?"

"As I said, I've got plans for him."

With the flash off, the tack room was a black hole. Gold lay handcuffed on the floor at Hy's feet. Hy let the silence build for nearly five minutes; it must've been an eternity for Gold. Then he turned on the light and shone it straight into the shackled man's eyes.

"For Christ's sake!" High-pitched, tremulous whine.

"If you believe in a god, better start praying."

The face twitched, pale in the blinding light.

"I'm going to ask you questions. You will respond truthfully. I already know the answers." He had learned these interrogation tactics in his early years with RKI, in order to extract information from people involved in hostage-holding situations.

He turned the flash out and waited.

John stirred restlessly behind him. Hy waited some more, until Gold began to moan, then switched on both the recorder and the flashlight. Gold flinched away from the glare, squeezed his eyes shut.

"Your name is Ben Gold?"

". . . Yes."

"You are the former lover of Larry Peeples?"

"What does this have to do—"

"Answer me."

"Yes."

"Did Larry Peeples tell you about Haven Dietz's plan to embezzle a hundred thousand dollars from her employer?"

No response.

"*Did* he?" Hy brought the light closer to Gold's face.

". . . Yes. He thought she'd never get away with it."

"How did you know she succeeded?"

"The night before she'd told Larry it was all set. Said she would bring her briefcase to his place, show him what real money looked like."

"The next night, did you attack her in the park and take the money from her briefcase?"

"No."

Hy brought the light to within an inch of Gold's closed eyelids. Gold rolled his head from side to side, moaning.

"*Did* you?"

"Okay, okay, yes."

"You hurt her badly. Was that necessary to subdue her?"

"She fought pretty hard."

"Did she?"

"Yes!"

"Tell me the truth, Gold."

"All right, I hated the bitch. She didn't like me, and I was afraid she'd convince Larry to dump me. I know people like her—they can't leave anybody alone. Her way or no way."

Hy shifted the light to one side. "So you brought the money here and concealed it under the floorboards."

". . . Yes. I was afraid it might be marked, or something."

"And when you decided it was safe to spend it, and that you and Larry could go away together . . . ?"

Silence.

"Gold?"

"All right. We fought. He was so smug, saying a hundred thousand wasn't much at all, saying that he was coming back here to run the vineyard."

"And you killed him?"

"No. He ran off—"

"The truth, Gold."

". . . I hit him. I hit him too hard and . . . he died."

"Where's his body?"

"I don't know. I left it in the alley behind the club we'd been drinking in."

Bullshit. The body of the son of a prominent vintner, who'd been reported missing, didn't go unidentified for months. Alicia Summers's body had, but the circumstances were entirely different.

Hy let it go for now.

"After you killed Larry, why did you leave the money here?"

". . . I couldn't start coming around right away; it might've made his folks suspicious."

"And why did you come for it tonight?"

"That detective, Julia Rafael, called me, wanting to talk again. I think she's on to something. I decided to grab the money and take off."

"Did Haven Dietz realize you were her attacker and demand something from you?"

"Something that she heard Julia Rafael say on the phone to Mrs. Peeples put it all together for her. She wanted the money. I was supposed to bring it to her apartment at six Sunday evening."

"But instead you killed her."

No response.

Hy moved the light again, and Gold squirmed.

"Did you?"

"Yes, yes, yes! Turn that light off! Please, turn it off!"

Hy didn't heed Gold's request. Instead, he asked, "Did you go to the offices of McCone Investigations on the night of Monday, July seventh, to look for the Dietz and Peeples files?"

No response.

He brought the light close in again. "Answer me."

Nothing.

Hy waited in silence until he heard a whimper.

"Are you ready to answer me now?"

"Yes! Yes, I went to the pier in the afternoon and hid there until everybody left and the guard was drinking. I was afraid of what might be in those files."

"But you couldn't access them, could you?"

"No."

"Did you shoot a woman who came into the office that you were searching?"

"I didn't know who she was, but I'd been to that pier before, and I was afraid she might recognize me. I panicked. I was trying to save myself."

"At my wife's expense."

Hy held the light on Gold's face a few seconds more, then switched it out. Said to John, "Turn on the overheads, would you? Let's get him out of here."

SHARON McCONE

They came through the door of my room—Hy and John, supporting a man between them. I knew from his photographs he was Ben Gold. A pair of concerned orderlies followed.

Hy turned to the orderlies, said, "Sorry, this is private business." Motioned for them to leave and shut the door.

Gold wore a buttoned-up coat. I could tell that under it he was handcuffed. The look on Gold's face was one of terror. Hy shoved him forward.

"There," Hy said, pushing him close to my bed. "See? That's what you've done to my wife!"

Gold closed his eyes. Hy shook him, forced his gaze onto mine. "I want you to see, dammit! This is what you did to her. I can also show you crime scene photos of Haven Dietz. You disfigured her for a hundred thousand dollars, then you killed her so you could keep the money."

Gold's mouth worked.

"Where's Larry's body?"

Rasping breaths, but no answer.

Hy said to Gold, "I'm asking you one more time. Where?"

"I . . . don't . . . know."

Hy hit him. Hit him hard enough to send him flying across the room and crashing into the wall. Gold slumped on the floor, gasping.

The orderlies were through the door now. John went to speak

with them while Hy took out his phone and speed-dialed. I listened as he talked to Adah.

"She'll contact the SFPD," he said after ending the call. "They like her a hell of a lot better than me."

The orderlies remained by the door, watchful.

I looked down at Gold. On his outflung arm I saw the gleam of the finely woven silver bracelet that had ultimately revealed him.

Metal grazing my fingers . . .

Flash!

Silver links in the brief, harsh light . . .

Falling . . .

Falling . . .

No. Not falling any more.

SUNDAY, SEPTEMBER 28

SHARON McCONE

It was my birthday—a perfect summer afternoon in San Francisco, even though the rest of the country was well into autumn. I sat in my wheelchair in a spot of sun on the deck, Alice the cat curled on my lap—she'd really become fond of this chair and the way we could zip around—watching Ralph stalk a bird in the backyard. He was getting old and slow and would never catch it.

No big party, no dinner out, no trip to Touchstone or the ranch. This year I'd opted for a quiet day and an intimate dinner at home with Hy. Most people who've been confined to hospitals for over two and a half months would've been aching for company, balloons, cake, champagne, presents—the works. But I'd had more company and excitement since I was shot than the average person does in a decade. Being right here, right now, with my husband cooking up something exotic in the kitchen was exactly where I wanted to be. I'd gone through the round of birthday calls and cards, e-mails and floral deliveries, and now here in the sun I felt pleasantly sleepy.

I'd come a long way in a short time, but I still had a long way to go. My doctors said my recovery was a miracle, and I certainly agreed. If I hadn't crashed when I did, needing immediate risky surgery, I might have remained cut off from the world for the rest of my life.

When you experience something that shattering, you realize

how casually we take all the givens—speech, motion, the ability to communicate with a glance or a gesture. The urge to make love, which last night had moved Hy and me to a successful conclusion. The ability to imagine a future.

A future that now didn't belong to a number of people: Harvey Davis; Amanda Teller; Paul Janssen; Larry Peeples, whose body had been found buried in a remote hilly section not far from his parents' vineyard; Haven Dietz; Ben Gold.

Although Gold disavowed the confession he'd made on tape to Hy—which wouldn't have been legally admissable anyway—he'd made one bad mistake. A .38-caliber Smith & Wesson Night Guard revolver registered to Larry Peeples had been found in the trunk of his car; the bullet that had killed Haven Dietz had been fired from it. There was no physical evidence he'd shot me—the bullet had been too fragmented—but at least he'd go down for Haven's murder. To my surprise, Gold had ignored his public defender's suggestion that he press charges against Hy and John for assault and kidnapping.

Hy's treatment of Gold had been harsh, but not as harsh as I'd feared. He hadn't crossed the line after all. I understood why he'd gone as far as he had. When someone nearly destroys your life, you hit back. I was certain that, if Gold's victim had been Hy, I would have done the same. And in a sense, that was what Gold had done when he lashed out and killed Larry Peeples: Larry had, after all, destroyed Ben's life by his refusal to go away with him.

I petted Allie and leaned my head back and let the sunlight play on my closed eyelids. Visions flashed on them.

SF General. Where I had almost died—twice.

The Brandt Institute, where I'd worked hard with the therapists so I could finally come home two days ago. Where I would continue to work daily toward a full and complete rehab.

Hy came onto the deck, carrying two champagne flutes. He stood in front of me, raised one glass.

I brushed Allie off my lap and got up, holding tightly to the ebony-and-brass tripod cane he'd gifted me with that morning. Took the other glass and looked into his eyes.

He said, "A wise man recently told me, '*Saika mukua kettae.* Her spirit is strong.' That was Elwood, and it turns out he knew what he was talking about.

"Happy birthday, warrior woman."